GRIZZLY MATE

MATEMATCH OUTCASTS BOOK 1

ARIANA HAWKES

Copyright ©2019 by Ariana Hawkes

All rights reserved. No part of this publication may be reproduced, distributed, or transmitted in any form or by any means, including photocopying, recording, or other electronic or mechanical methods, without the prior written permission of the publisher, except in the case of brief quotations embodied in critical reviews and certain other noncommercial uses permitted by copyright law.

This is a work of fiction. Names, characters, businesses, places, events and incidents are either the products of the author's imagination or used in a fictitious manner. Any resemblance to actual persons, living or dead, or actual events and businesses is purely coincidental.

ISBN: 9798682164134

CHAPTER 1

The late-afternoon sun sat low over the desolate mountain town, and it was getting harder to see. Savannah squinted into the pale light, one hand clamped to her forehead, as she trudged up and down endless dirt roads, checking each house against the image on her phone.

She was hot and dusty and tired, and her feet ached like crazy, but she couldn't think about any of that right now. Her mate was here somewhere, amid these forbidding, dark-wood houses, and she had to find him before it got dark.

Which wasn't very far off.

A little knot of nerves in her stomach was spreading like a prickly rash, raising the hairs on the back of her neck and filling her with foreboding. This wasn't the peaceful rural town she'd expected, but a broken-down, half-abandoned ghost town. Everything about it told her to run back to her car and get the hell away.

But she couldn't.

Because it was all she had left.

She went on, holding up her phone, comparing tiny details of windows and door frames. She'd thought it was weird that the matchmaking service had sent her a picture of Garrett's house instead of an address, but now she got it: there were no street names or numbers. Just one beat-up museum relic after another; all rotting dark-wood sidings, darkened windows. They all looked alike, but none of them matched the photo exactly. And she was fast running out of options.

Gusts of wind rolled through the deserted streets, kicking up dust and stinging her eyes. Everything said lonely. She wrapped her arms around her body, fortifying herself against it. Loneliness she was used to. It was what had brought her here in the first place. The kind of soul-destroying loneliness that eats up a person from the inside, until all that's left is a raw, scraped-out shell. She knew it so well, it almost felt like home.

Which was why she wasn't going to quit now. She was going to find one of those mean-eyed people she'd seen hurrying along the street, shooting her hostile glances, and ask them for help. She'd been shy to approach them, but she was about ready to throw her last scrap of caution to the winds.

But now, there wasn't a single soul in sight. It was just her and the dust and the wind. There *was* a wooden shack at the end of the road though, and there seemed to be something written across the front in what looked like spray paint. She hurried up to it. *Bar* was stenciled across the battered wooden siding in faded purple paint, but it had been crossed out, with what actually was spray paint, and *Last Chans Saloon* was scrawled on top.

She snorted. "Very appropriate," she muttered to herself. The place looked to be on the verge of collapse. It had been knocked together from a bunch of mismatched planks, and its rusted metal porch was barely supported by a couple of twisted sapling trunks. There was only one window, which was half covered in duct tape, while the other two panes were coated in a film of orange dust. Swallowing hard, she walked up and peered through. But as she pressed her face closer, a rumble of voices rose up, and then a much louder noise erupted, rattling the glass.

She gasped and jumped back, her heart pounding. What *was* that? Something between a snarl and a roar, it sounded more animal than a human. A big dog? *Crap.* She was terrified of big dogs, and this one sounded like it could eat her alive. She couldn't see a thing through the windows, but the voices were louder than before; all rough and growly and unwelcoming. She stared at the battered front door. Its glass panels were boarded up, as if to deter curious eyes. Walking into this place was the dead last thing she wanted to do. But she had to at least try. Steeling herself, she took hold of the rusty door handle and gave it a good tug.

The door creaked open, the rotted wooden boards scraping on the floor. It was dim inside, and suddenly very quiet. It took a moment for her eyes to adjust to the light, then her heart jumped into her mouth at the sight of half a dozen men glaring at her with cold, feral eyes. Something bumped her ass and she yelped.

Calm down. It was only the door closing. She backed up against it, took some deep breaths to slow her heartbeat and took in the room. The air was hot and thick and full of a pungent animal smell that made her wrinkle her nose. *Shifters.* Of course, they were. Of course, Garrett wasn't the only shifter in town. They were all sitting separately, like they couldn't stand each other; two on high stools at the bar, and the others on plastic crates dotted around the room. The one nearest the door let off a snarl. He was huge and meaty, with a scraggy brown beard and different colored eyes—one icy blue, the other impenetrable black.

Savannah didn't need to speak man-beast to interpret him. He meant *get the hell out of here.* The hairs on the back of her neck prickled again in warning, but she squared her shoulders and took two steps into the room. She'd seen her fair share of beasts in her life, and these men weren't about to scare her. Her feet crunched on peanut shells and broken glass.

A bartender emerged from the shadows. Slapping two huge hands on the bartop, he stared her down. He had a heavy beard and fierce yellow eyes with weirdly dilated pupils. He was massive as well. *What was it with this town—were all the shifters on growth hormone or something?*

"Need something?" he grunted.

She took another two steps and laid her fingertips on the bar, delicately, letting him know she wasn't about to be intimidated. "Know where Garrett's house is?"

He scowled. "What d'you want with him?"

None of your damn business. "I've got a meeting with him," she said instead, and despite the lump in her throat, her voice came through strong and clear.

He huffed, picked up a couple of glasses and dumped them on a shelf behind the bar.

"Can you just explain how to get to his place?" she persisted.

"Garrett's the last person you should be looking for," came a low voice from the left side of the room. Its owner was hunched over his beer, in a gray wife-beater, with sleeve tattoos on both arms. His ass was on a leather jacket, and he was wearing black biker boots. With his spiked-up brown hair and startling green eyes, he was hot, or he would've been, if he hadn't been looking at her with such menace. He spoke soft, but it was one of those voices that carried a long way.

"Says who?" she demanded.

"Says me, little girl." He eyed her curves in a way she didn't much like. "He'll eat you for breakfast." He snapped his teeth together. "So would I."

A shiver went down her spine, but she planted a hand on her ample hip and affected a bored tone. "I wouldn't bank on it. Not if he's anything like you guys."

"Is that an insult?"

"Well, it's not a compliment." She ran her eyes over him deliberately.

His frozen-lake eyes widened. "Now I'm hurt."

"You should be. A real man doesn't talk to a woman like that."

He sneered. "We're hardly men, baby."

She gulped. He was right. All of them were at least seventy-five percent beast.

She forced out a sigh. "Are you going to help me or not?"

Seven blank stares greeted her question.

"Fine. Screw you all." She turned on her heel and shoved the door open. To her right, meaty, snarling guy caught her eye and gave a warning shake of his head. Ignoring him, she stepped outside and let the door bang behind her.

Savannah was shaking all over as she walked back to her old red sedan, which, thank the heavens, was still where she'd left it. Every last thing she owned was inside it. Was Garrett like those beasts? From what the asshole at the bar had been saying, he was worse. If that was true…well, that would be a lot. She didn't expect much from her match. She didn't even care what he looked like, as long as he was decent and didn't have two heads or something. Garrett had sounded nice in his dating profile. A bear shifter—protective and loyal, and that was enough for her. But no way could she share her life with another beast. That, she'd tried already.

She opened the door and was halfway onto the seat when a tall figure appeared right beside her. She yelped, yanked the door shut and hit the lock. His face was hidden in shadow, but his eyes burned with the same feral fire of the beast-men in the bar. He was in his late fifties, with craggy skin and long, tangled gray hair. When he tapped on the glass, she shrank back, the handbrake jabbing her in the hip.

"This is no place for you," he rasped. "Go!"

She whimpered, hugging herself.

"Go!" he repeated again and again, jabbing the window with a yellowed index finger. "Go!"

"Leave me the hell alone!" she bawled.

At last, he shook his head, turned and lumbered off, like a huge, shambling beast.

Savannah eased herself fully onto the seat, breathing fast and rubbing her perspiring face. She didn't know how much more of this she could take. Every last person she'd met was warning her off this town. Was she dumb to ignore them?

Most probably.

And yet, she had nowhere else to be. The thought was so desperate that it weighed down on her chest, making it hard to breathe.

How could she leave without at least setting eyes on her match? On this guy that the matchmaker insisted was right for her? She shook her arms and legs to loosen the tension in her body.

One more try.

She'd drive around the town this time. There were some places on the outskirts that she hadn't checked. She started up the car and drove slowly down what passed for the main street. The road was more pothole than surface and the orange dust rose up in thick clouds. At the far end, she made a right, and then a left onto a road she hadn't yet seen. Or at least, she didn't think she'd seen it. All those beat-up facades looked the same, untouched for a century or more. It was as if the current inhabitants had decided to leave the town just as it was, last occupied circa the Gold Rush.

She passed a couple more men who were prowling along, shoulders hunched, eyes darting from side to side. She hadn't seen a single woman yet. That was weird. A creepy town full of terrifying man-beasts, and nothing else. Still, it was an improvement on the life she'd left behind.

The house at the end of the road looked familiar. She pressed on her brake, pulled her phone out and held it up. For the hundredth time that day, she compared the photo from MateMatch with the building in front of her.

It was large, with a double frontage; a little dilapidated and in need of repairs, but she could see it had been built well, and the front door and steps were brand new. In short, it was exactly like the picture. Butterflies fluttered in her stomach. She parked up, pulled down the vanity mirror and checked her appearance. Her mascara was still in place, somehow, bringing out the deep blue of her eyes, which everyone said was her best feature. But her long, golden blonde hair was tousled and messy from the wind that had been howling nonstop. She grabbed her hairbrush from her purse and did her best to straighten it out. Then she took three long, slow breaths and got out of the car.

Savannah walked up the four wooden steps on trembling legs.

There was no doorbell or knocker, so she rapped on the glass panel, then the wooden frame, as the breeze swirled around her.

After a long pause, the door began to open. Her heart skittered beneath her ribcage like a trapped bird.

A tall, broad shouldered man filled the doorway, and she stifled a laugh of surprise.

He definitely didn't have two heads. In fact, he was as sexy as sin, all slanting cheekbones and square jaw, with eyes like brown pools beneath thick, straight eyebrows and cropped dark hair. Her knees literally went weak.

He looked her up and down and something flashed in his eyes; something fierce and yearning. But it disappeared as fast as it had come, shuttered away behind a cold, questioning glare.

"At last!" she exclaimed. "You're not an easy man to find. I'm Savannah." When he didn't react, she stuck her hand out, but he didn't take it. Instead, he continued to stare at her.

"Your match," she prompted, with a girlish laugh that she regretted immediately.

He frowned, and her stomach dropped. He was disappointed with her. So disappointed that he couldn't bring himself to speak.

"What do you need?" he said in a deep, rumbling voice.

"Uhhh, t-to meet you. To spend some time together. G-get to know each other a little," she stammered, wringing her hands together. "See if we're right for each other."

This was awful, even worse than she'd expected. Of course, she'd considered the fact that he might not like what he saw, but the matchmaker had reassured her that she was just his type. Pretty and curvy and gutsy enough for him. Obviously not. Her cheeks burned.

He cleared his throat. "Miss, I have no idea what you're talking about, and to be honest, I'm kind of busy."

She wrung her hands tighter. "We've been matched on MateMatch. The matchmaker showed me your ad and confirmed we were a match. And then she forwarded me your photo of the house because you don't have a door number—" she broke off, because he was looking at her like she was certifiably insane.

"Matchmaker…photo…what? You're at the wrong house." The crease in his forehead got deeper. "Although, I doubt there's a right house for you in this town."

She pursed her lips. "You are Garrett?"

"Yup. But how do you know my name?"

She sighed. "Because you're my match. I already explained—"

He took a step forward, which brought him over the threshold, and she quailed. He really was a big guy. Again, there was that cold look in his eye, as if he could rip her to pieces without thinking about it. "Garrett's my name, as well as the name of many other people. You've got the wrong person, and you should leave."

"I get it, I get it." She held her hands up, doing her best to ignore the barb of rejection that was currently stabbing her in the heart. "You don't like me. This was a wasted journey."

"Lady, this isn't about liking you or not liking you," he said through gritted teeth. "You've got the wrong person. Either that, or you're crazy."

"Crazy?" Anger rolled through her. "I might be a lot of things, but crazy isn't one of them. I have your name. I have a photo of your house." She brandished her phone and jabbed a finger at the screen. Then she went very still. "But I'm starting to think this is all a joke. And I didn't drive all the way up here, with everything I own in my trunk to be the butt of someone's joke!"

Garrett made a noise low in his throat. He was massive, towering over her, and every instinct told her to back up. But if she did that, she'd most likely take a tumble down the stairs.

"I'm not joking," he said, speaking very slowly. "And I'm definitely not looking for a mate."

Savannah stared at him with a mixture of misery and confusion. She was supposed to be walking into her new life, but instead she seemed to be the victim of a very mean practical joke. What else was there for her to do but leave? Drive all the way back to a place she'd planned never to see again? The thought made her insides crumple like a paper bag.

"You shouldn't be making a dating profile if you're not looking for a mate," she told him. "It might be a joke to you, but it's not a joke to me." Her emotions welled up and she quickly turned her face away. This brought her car into view, which was sitting low on its suspension, heavily loaded with her possessions. She took a couple of deep breaths. "Whatever. I'm not going to try to convince a man who's clearly not interested. Been there, done that, and it didn't turn out well for me. I'm not going through it again."

Garrett scanned her face and his hostility dissolved into outright confusion. "I'm sorry you were misled," he said in a softer tone. "But I definitely didn't post any ads on any matchmaking service. As I said, I'm not looking for a mate."

Savannah nodded. She'd tried her best, but a girl needed to know when she was beat. "It's fine. I'm done here. I'm going to go check into a hotel."

She turned around and, on heavy legs, she trudged down the stairs and returned to her car, disappointment weighing on her shoulders.

CHAPTER 2

*G*arrett watched as the cute, curvy, crazy lady retreated, her pretty golden hair billowing in the evening breeze. Thank Christ she'd finally gotten the message and was leaving him in peace. He went back into his house and slammed the door behind him.

Then he stopped.

He turned and yanked the door open again. "There are no hotels in town," he called.

The woman had climbed into the driver's seat and was on the point of shutting her door. "I'll just drive to the nearest one I find." Her voice was tight and cold.

He sighed. "There are no hotels nearby either."

Her eyes widened. "Seriously?"

He shrugged. "No tourists. No passing trade. No need."

Her mouth opened and closed. "I guess I'll just drive back down…" She trailed off and he knew she was thinking of the poorly maintained mountain road that led down from Ragtown, and the back roads that led on from it. It would be dark before she got halfway down the mountain.

"You can stay at my place tonight," he blurted out. "But just for one night."

Her eyes got very big. "No, it's fine. I'll camp out in my car."

"No!" he almost shouted. "Ragtown can get wild after dark. It's not even safe for a lone woman to be walking around the town."

It was the truth. She was tough, and obviously didn't take any crap, which appealed to his bear a lot more than it should have. But Ragtown was Ragtown. It was definitely not a place for humans; it was barely a place for shifters. It was a no man's land, inhabited by broken, deranged souls, each a half-step away from being put out of their misery.

"I've been in the bar," she muttered, as if speaking to herself, and wrapped her arms around her body.

"That's Ragtown," he said simply. "It's not for humans, and no one likes outsiders."

She peered up at his house and all the fight seemed to go out of her. "I guess I'll stay the night, then. Thank you." She swung the car door open and climbed out again.

"Need help bringing your luggage inside?"

She glanced at the trunk and gave a mirthless laugh. "You'd be busy for a while. Will it be okay here overnight?"

"Yeah. No one here's real... materialistic, if you know what I mean. If you had beer in there, it'd be a different story though." He laughed and she joined in, too, but like she was being polite, not because she thought it was funny. It wasn't funny, really. All shifters did here was fight and drown their sorrows.

"I'll just grab my overnight bag." She retrieved a hot pink holdall from the rear seats and locked the doors. She looked upset as she followed him into the house, keeping her head down low, her hair falling over her face. He guessed he didn't blame her. Somehow, she'd gotten the idea that she was coming here to meet the man of her dreams. How ironic that she'd been set up with him. He was more the stuff of nightmares. The earlier she left tomorrow, the better.

The house was hardly suitable for guests. Like all the houses in

Ragtown, it had been abandoned for a long time, and he was slowly fixing it up, but a lot of the wood was rotten. He wasn't about to apologize for it, though.

Luckily, the kids were still at an age where they loved sharing a bedroom, so he had a spare room for her to sleep in at the back of the house. He flung the door open and showed her in. The twin bed wasn't made up, but the mattress was new.

She shook her head, as if coming to her senses. "It's great. Thank you. I appreciate this."

"It's fine. It's a spare room. No one else uses it." *Damn.* He hadn't meant to say that, in case it encouraged her to stay longer, but she looked so forlorn. She went over to the bed and sat down heavily, letting her bag fall to the floor. She'd had a hard time. What had she been saying about other men abandoning her? And now someone was playing some kind of mean trick on her, too? She was a good person, he sensed it deep in his bones. She deserved a good man who would take care of her, so she didn't have to be so tough and self-reliant.

His stomach growled. It was round about dinnertime. She must be hungry, too. He wished he could get takeout, but there was nowhere to eat in town. He was just going to have to be hospitable until she left. He could do that much. His bear purred its approval, and he shushed it up. It had nothing to do with the fact that she was smoking hot, with killer curves. He was just being decent, was all.

"You hungry?" he said.

She lifted her gaze from the floor. Her eyes were bright blue—like the ocean, or perfect summer skies, or cornflowers. But they were full of sadness, and that saddened him, too. Made his bear turn over inside him. "I'm really tired and I just want to sleep," she murmured.

"Okay. I'll leave you to it." He pulled the door closed. It didn't shut fully because the frame was warped, leaving an inch of space along the side. He hoped she didn't mind.

As he went to the kitchen to figure out what he was going to make, Holt hurtled into the room. "Who's that lady?" he shrilled in his seven-year-old's voice.

Garrett reached out and tousled his mop of shiny brown hair. "Which lady?" he asked innocently.

Holt rolled his big brown eyes dramatically. "The one you just let into the house and put in the empty bedroom. I might be a kid, but I'm not stupid, Garrett."

Garrett turned his head away and grinned. "Nope. You're a whole lot smarter than I am. She's just a friend, who's staying for the night. So, we've got to be hospitable to her."

"Hospitable…?"

"Make her feel welcome."

Holt frowned and held his hands out, palms up. "Of course, durr. That's what you do when you've got guests."

"And that's what makes you smarter than me, kid." Garrett opened the sole kitchen cupboard and rummaged through it. They had staples like rice and pasta, and there was a small vegetable patch out the back, but most of their diet was meat that he'd hunted in the forest. Did she even know he was a shifter? And would she freak out if he disappeared and returned with a bunch of rabbits? He frowned at a jar of marinara sauce. He could do pasta sauce and throw some leftover meat in it, maybe.

As he was filling up the kettle, Opal and Poppy scampered into the kitchen, giggling. "What's funny, Squirts?" he asked automatically. Giggling usually meant that mischief followed close behind.

"We saw the lady!" Poppy stage-whispered.

"She's really pretty," Opal said, a lot louder.

Garrett groaned. "Have you been in her room?" he demanded.

"No! We just looked through the gap in the door," Opal said, full of self-righteousness.

He could just imagine how subtle they'd been. He flicked the kettle on and went to the spare room, treading on light feet.

The woman met him at the door, her eyes sleepy.

"Sorry."

"It's okay. I'm getting up. Your kids are cute." She smiled blurrily.

"They're not—" he began, but stopped himself. There was no need to explain the whole story to her. Come tomorrow, he'd never see her again. "Faces of angels, souls of wild little bear cubs," he said instead.

"They're also bear shifters?" she said hesitantly, as he showed her into the kitchen.

"Yup. All three of them. Meet Holt, and the twins, Poppy and Opal."

"We're five," Opal said, lacing her chubby little fingers together and tipping her head back so she could look the woman in the eye. "But I'm the oldest."

Poppy sighed loudly and stomped her foot. "By three minutes!"

The woman giggled. He was relieved that she evidently liked kids.

Holt went over to her and stuck out his hand, and she shook it solemnly. "I'm seven if that's important to you."

"I'm Savannah, and I'm twenty-nine," she said.

"Garrett's thirty-four," Poppy said.

"Okay. Everyone knows everyone's ages." Garrett clapped his hands together. "Savannah, take a seat at the table while I make dinner." Nice name, he thought. It suited her.

"I'll help," Holt volunteered. He was always quick to offer help, as if he thought he owed Garret something. He didn't. Garrett was more than happy to take care of the three of them. He owed them more than they'd ever know.

Obediently, Savannah sat down at the table, and the twins each dragged a chair up on either side of her and clambered up, eager to get as close to her as possible.

"Guys! Give the poor woman a bit of space. You're stealing her air," Garrett chided them, but they just giggled.

He opened the fridge and started sorting through the meat, trying to decide which went best with pasta sauce.

"Do you know how to make cake?" A small voice stage-whispered. "Garrett doesn't. He tried once but he wasn't very good."

Garrett whirled around. Poppy was standing up on her chair, her hands cupped around Savannah's ear, while Savannah was grinning at him mischievously. Inexplicably, there was a twinge in his chest.

"Sorry," Poppy said, flashing Garrett a guilty look. "But cake is my favorite dish in the world."

"Mine's pizza," Opal said. "What's yours?"

Savannah looked dreamy. "I love pizza and cake, too. But steak is my favorite. Actually, if you have the ingredients, I could make pizza and cake tonight—if that's okay with you?" She directed the question at Garrett.

Garrett scanned her features. She looked weary, with blue shadows under her eyes. She was obviously trying to be a good sport. "Guys, Savannah is tired. I'll try to make you a better cake next time," he said.

"It's okay. I can make a cake." She shrugged. "Baking relaxes me."

He felt like an ass. He'd been mean to her on the doorstep, and now here she was, being kind to his kids. "I'm not sure if we have the right stuff. There's no grocery store in the town. We just get deliveries of the basics every now and then."

She got to her feet. "Will I be intruding if I look in your cupboard?"

"No, go for it."

With what looked like eagerness, she went to the cupboard and opened the door and rummaged inside. "Yeah, it's all here," she said after a moment. She pulled a bunch of things out and put them on the counter.

"You sure you're up to this?" Garrett said, looking at her sideways. "You don't need to make a good impression."

"Of course. It'll be the best part of my day so far." She flashed him a smile. Then she washed her hands and got to work right away.

With nothing to do now, Garrett sat down at the kitchen table. It had been a long day of work and he was also tired.

"Let's play animal charades?" Opal piped up.

"Good plan!" he said injecting some brightness into his voice. Immediately, the three children started acting out all kinds of mind-boggling animal impressions with much hilarity. When it was Opal's second turn, she flapped around the kitchen, making ridiculous noises, but in vain. No one could guess her animal.

"I think it's a bee," Savannah said over her shoulder.

"Yes!" Opal exclaimed and started buzzing.

Garrett pressed his hands to his forehead. "Why didn't you do that in the first place?" he groaned.

"It would've been too easy!" Opal said, and Savannah laughed loudly. He glanced at her rear view, which was very appealing in a pair of stretchy black pants and a fitted lilac shirt; all hips and sweet curvy ass. He liked her more by the minute. Which was the last thing he needed to be thinking.

When the cake dough and pizza were ready, he helped her with the oven, then she joined them at the table. Her cheeks were a little flushed, and her eyes were sparkling. She was even prettier than before. He worked his jaw back and forth. Having her here was getting his bear all stirred up, and keeping it under control was severely testing his nerves. He sprang to his feet. "How about we grab a drink and go sit out the back?" he suggested.

The kids whooped in agreement.

"Sure," Savannah said.

He opened the fridge door, took out three sodas and passed them to the kids. "Beer?" he said, looking at Savannah over his shoulder.

"Great," she said with relief in her voice. Maybe she was tenser than he'd thought.

They went around to the back of the house, where there was a small terrace looking onto a stream and the nearby mountain peak. Ragtown was almost at the summit, but an area of higher ground provided some protection from the elements.

"This is really nice," Savannah said, taking a seat on a thick slice of tree trunk that Garrett pulled out for her.

"Yeah I love it here. It's safe from all the craziness of Ragtown. The only place I'd let the kids play after sundown."

"Do you have any kids?" Holt butted in.

"I don't," she said, and there was that sadness in her eyes again. Garrett had the feeling she'd be a good mom, and for the second time that day he hoped she'd meet a mate soon.

"You're an orphan, too," Opal said.

Savannah's lips parted and her eyebrows drew together questioningly.

"We don't have a mom, and you don't have kids," Opal supplied.

"Ohh, I'm sorry to hear that," she said cautiously, flashing Garrett a glance. He nodded, telling her it was okay. "Actually, an orphan is just where you don't have parents. I grew up without a mom myself, but luckily I had a great dad, and I was fine."

"Garrett isn't our real dad, but he's the best," Poppy said, laying her small, hot hand on his knee, and the other two agreed enthusiastically. Garrett's heart clenched, and he swigged his beer.

The kids continued chattering away about themselves, and asking Savannah lots of inappropriate questions that she batted away efficiently, and he fell silent, content to take a break from the responsibilities of parenthood. He was also eager to ask Savannah questions, to find out what had brought her to this last-hope town, intent on getting mated to someone she'd never met. But he had no reason to get to know her any better. She'd be gone tomorrow, and the less he knew about her, the faster she'd be gone from his mind.

"Okay, dinner should be about ready," Savannah said after a while. Holt, Poppy and Opal cheered. Judging by the smells filtering from the kitchen, it was going to be tasty.

As they left the terrace, the nocturnal sounds from Ragtown were starting up—the howls and snarls of beasts, accompanied by the endless brawling. Garrett shook his head, glad his charges were safely inside—and that included Savannah. He couldn't have lived with himself if she'd fled his hostility and something had happened to her in the town.

The pizza was delicious, with a nice, thick crust, piled high with a variety of meats.

"This is the best pizza I've ever had," Poppy said through a mouthful of food.

"Yeah!" Holt agreed.

"Thanks, guys," Savannah said, looking pleased and relieved.

"You should come and live here," Opal said.

Savannah gave a choked laugh. "Oh, no, I couldn't," she said.

"Why not?" Poppy insisted.

"Because she doesn't belong here," Garrett said firmly. Hurt swept across Savannah's features and he instantly regretted his words. But they'd burst out of his mouth because they were true. She was only here because of him, and it was all a big mistake.

CHAPTER 3

Savannah got out of bed and peeked through the curtains of the bedroom where she'd slept the previous night. The sky was pale gray, and the mountain peak was still dark and forbidding. It was just after six a.m., and she'd slept surprisingly well. Probably because she'd felt safe, she realized with a shock. It was the first time she'd felt like that for a long time. Garrett was a stranger to her, and he'd made it abundantly clear that there was no room for her in his life, but she trusted him. He blew hot and cold, hostile and kind, but the way he took care of what were evidently someone else's kids proved he was a decent person. She'd had fun last night, cooking and looking after everyone. And after the kids had gone to bed and Garrett was washing the dishes, she'd longed to ask him how he'd come to be their guardian, but it was none of her business.

She pulled on a fresh set of clothes and brushed her hair, listening all the time. The house was quiet. If she left now, hopefully she could sneak out before Garrett and the children were up. Already, it would be hard saying goodbye to Holt, Poppy and Opal. And Garrett... she was no closer to understanding why she'd been matched with him, when he obviously knew nothing about it, but the sad part was that he was a perfect match—for her anyway. A hundred times better than the guy she'd expected to meet. Not only was he loyal, protective, and caring, but he was the most handsome man she'd ever laid eyes on. That serious, good-natured expression. Those fathomless eyes that seemed to look right into her soul. Those little crinkles that appeared at the corners of his eyes when he broke into one of his rare smiles. Her throat tightened. He didn't want a mate. She couldn't blame him. He was a great father and could definitely take care of the children by himself. And she had to respect that.

But where did that leave her? She was supposed to be finding her forever-mate. And now she was back to square one. Actually, square minus-one, because now she was going to have to get over Garrett before she was ready to meet someone else. Maybe she should look for the matchmaking agency in town and asked them what had happened. Perhaps they'd mixed his profile up with someone else's. He said he'd never applied to the matchmaking service though. *Or maybe he was lying, and the truth was that he didn't like what he saw when he opened the door to you,* a mean little voice said.

The thought hurt. With a final glance around the room, Savannah picked up her holdall, eased the door open and crept out of the room.

Only fifteen feet to the front door. She went fast, on tiptoes.

"Savannah!" cried a little voice when she passed the kitchen door.

Her heart sank. Garrett was standing in the middle of the kitchen, wearing a blue plaid shirt, half-unbuttoned, and carrying Poppy on his hip. He looked rumpled from sleep, and even more gorgeous than the night before.

"Hi," she said weakly.

His forehead furrowed in confusion. "You're not leaving?"

"Yeah. Thought I'd get an early start."

"You've got to have breakfast first. It's the most important meal of the day!" Poppy shrilled.

Garrett smiled at the little girl tenderly, and a twinge hit Savannah in the chest.

"Poppy's right," he said, directing his attention to Savannah with a smile so sexy that it lit her up inside. "But we'll have to wake the others up. This one here is an early bird at the moment, so we usually get up and have some time to ourselves first thing."

Savannah smiled at them. It was so sweet that he did that. She recalled her own childhood, where early awakenings were greeted with anger and frustration, rather than understanding.

"No, it's okay. I should go," she said with reluctance, suddenly wanting to be part of this cozy family breakfast routine.

"You have to stay!" Poppy exclaimed and started wriggling in Garrett's arms. Obligingly, he put her down, and she hurtled off. In another moment, Opal sprinted into the room in a unicorn night dress, followed by Holt in red pajamas, yawning. Opal immediately flung her arms around Savannah's waist and hugged her tight, while Holt waved at her amiably.

"Looks like you're staying," Garrett said in an even tone. His expression was neutral, and she didn't know whether he was agreeable, or secretly annoyed.

"We're having the best cake in the world for breakfast," Opal announced. Savannah's cake had already been the subject of much praise last night, and there was a little less than half of it left.

"And that's where you're mistaken, Squirt," Garrett said, squatting down and laying his hands on Opal's tiny shoulders. "We're having eggs for breakfast. Cake in the afternoon, maybe, if you're all good."

"Okay, if I'm staying, I'm making breakfast," Savannah said and headed for the fridge.

Garrett insisted on sharing the work with her, and together they made scrambled eggs on toast. He was obviously used to doing things his own way, but she had the impression he was glad for her help.

It was a small but homely kitchen, with a big, wooden table that looked like it had been there as long as the house. The dark-wood cupboard and counters were similarly rustic, but the fridge and stove were new.

"Are you going to be our new mommy?" Poppy demanded, as they sat down to breakfast. Savannah's gut lurched and automatically, her gaze flicked over to Garrett, just in time to catch the displeasure in his eyes. He didn't look mad though. There was something else there…maybe regret. He was probably thinking about the children's mother.

"No, honey, I'm just Garrett's friend. That's all." Keeping her head down, she busied herself with cutting up Opal's food into smaller pieces, while Garrett did the same with Poppy's.

When they'd finished eating, Garrett clapped his hands together. "Right, kids, time to get ready for school."

They bounced off excitedly, and Savannah threw him a questioning glance, surprised that Ragtown was big enough to contain a school.

"That's school in inverted commas," Garrett explained, taking the dishes over to the sink. "It's actually in the town's library. Florence, the librarian, takes care of them during the day while I'm at work, and gives them some lessons."

"That's nice," she said, and she ran her eyes over his big forearms and broad shoulders as he worked. Guys who didn't want a mate shouldn't be allowed to be as sexy as him. "I was thinking I'd leave once they're gone so they don't get upset?"

He glanced at her and nodded. "Good idea. The door's on the latch, so you can just close it after us." His tone was even, but there was that look in his eyes again, of regret, or something else.

She cleared her throat, which suddenly felt tight. "I'd better say now, thanks for putting me up last night, after I randomly turned up on your doorstep."

"You're welcome." He frowned. "Where will you go now?"

"To the agency. To figure out what went wrong."

He nodded seriously. "I hope it goes well. And that, you know, you get the mate you deserve."

The mate you deserve. What did he mean by that? Savannah's stomach lurched again and for a terrible moment, she thought she was going to be sick. But then Holt rushed into the room, asking where his green dinosaur T-shirt was, and the words seemed to hang in the air.

The kids said goodbye at the door. Opal and Poppy wrapped their arms around her and thanked her for the cake and the pizza. Holt told her that he liked the cake and pizza too, and he shook her hand. "Girls hug and boys shake hands, Garrett says," he explained.

When the kids' attention was distracted, Garrett whispered goodbye to her, and their eyes met one last time.

"Goodbye," she managed to reply, and their front door closed, leaving her alone in the hallway.

She put her hands over her face and counted to a hundred, and then she picked up her bag, walked outside and unlocked the car door.

The mountain air was chilly this early in the morning, and it shocked her out of the emotion that had been welling up inside her. She'd known the four of them for so little time; how could their company have affected her so much?

Because they were a family, she realized as she started up the car. And she hadn't had the feeling of being among family for a long, long time.

And because their adoptive father was exactly the kind of guy she wanted to be her mate. But the sooner she put that idea out of her head, the better.

She began to drive through the town slowly, just as she'd done yesterday, but this time she was looking for the MateMatch agency sign. The town seemed no more welcoming in the morning light. The streets were still deserted, aside from an occasional man lurking in the shadows or scurrying along, casting furtive glances around. *Shifters,* she corrected herself. She'd understood from Garrett last night that this was an exclusively shifter town, and she was likely the only human here. *Fresh meat.* The phrase popped into her head, and she shivered. What would've happened if she'd tried to sleep in her car last night? She dismissed the thought fast.

She went up and down all the streets, two times over, but there was no sign of MateMatch. In fact, there were no signs in town at all.

Maybe there was something in the emails she'd received from the agency. She parked up on the main street, at the opposite end from Last Chans Saloon, took her phone out and opened the email app.

There was a rap on her window. She jumped and her head jerked up, to be greeted by the sight of one of the assholes she'd seen yesterday. The one who'd been sitting at the bar, making crude comments. He rotated his finger, indicating she should open the window, but she scowled at him, sure that nothing he could say would be welcome.

But then…he might know something about the agency. Unlikely as it seemed, what other option did she have? She cracked her window open an inch, and he broke into a grin. He had nice teeth for someone so feral-looking, she noted distractedly.

"Still in town, huh?" He eyed the passenger seats, which were packed high with boxes. "Must've been a rough night."

She shrugged noncommittally.

"Not one to listen to other people are you?"

"Looks like we share that in common," she retorted.

He laughed, and suddenly, she glimpsed an okay-guy behind all that crudeness and posturing.

"I'm Aidan. I like you," he said.

"I'm glad. Happen to know where the MateMatch office is?"

His eyes widened. "MateMatch, you say? What's that?"

"It's a matchmaking agency," she explained.

He puffed his cheeks out. "Must be a matchmaking agency from hell if it sent you to Ragtown, doll." His smile turned sly. "What are your sins?"

She sighed. "Plenty. But that's not the point."

He grinned and tilted his head to the side. "I can tell you're a naughty girl."

"I'm not a girl. I'm a woman," she snapped.

"Ooooh...!" He threw his head back and made a sound like a wolf's howl. "Like that feistiness. I'm available if you're looking for a mate." He flashed a winning smile.

"I wouldn't mate a wolf," she said tersely.

He nodded slowly, impressed. "A wolf. You got me."

Someone appeared behind him. A huge, intimidating someone, with massive shoulders, a bushy beard that covered most of his face, and long dark hair, tied up in a bun. "You causing trouble again, Aidan?" he demanded. When he bent down to peer at Savannah through the window, she was surprised that his brown eyes were soft and almost friendly, although a long scar cut through his right eyebrow, hitching it up at the outer edge.

"You're just jealous because you don't know how to talk to girls, bro," Aidan said, clapping him on the shoulder.

"If that's something you want to learn, you should stay away from him," Savannah told brown eyes.

"That's not nice." Aidan jammed his hands in his pockets and scowled.

Savannah ran her gaze over the other guy. She had the impression he was more likely to help than Aidan. "Know where I can find the MateMatch agency?" she asked him.

He tugged at his beard and frowned thoughtfully. "Haven't heard of any agency," he muttered. "But...if there's someone who'll know about it, it's Florence."

"The librarian?" Savannah supplied.

"Settling in well for someone who just got to town," Aidan piped up. "A woman with a mission, I like that." He planted his hands on his hips. "The offer still stands, baby."

"Cut the crap, Aidan," the other guy snapped. "The library is on the main street, half way down on the left. It's the one with the new pine siding," he told Savannah.

"Thanks. Why did you do that?"

"Why did I do what?" he asked in his deep, rumbling voice.

"Step in when this guy was giving me shit." She cocked her head at Aidan.

He shrugged. "Guess you remind me of my sister. She didn't know how to stay out of trouble either."

She rolled her eyes. "Seems to follow me around."

"I'm Jagger." He bent close to the crack in the window. "Let me know if you get in any trouble here."

"I appreciate that. I'm Savannah." She thanked him again and started up the car. Ragtown was like nowhere she'd been before, she thought as she turned the car around and got ready to drive down Main Street again. Aidan was a sleazy troublemaker, but she could tell there was a good heart behind his immature façade. Jagger was kind, but she sensed he was troubled, and those soft eyes were full of torment. This town seemed to be a place for broken people, and that might just be where she belonged.

CHAPTER 4

Savannah followed Jagger's directions to the library. It was right there, where he'd said it would be. The bright, pine frontage stood out in a street of dark wood sidings, and couple of tables and chairs were set in front of it, along with a blackboard sign advertising coffee, cake and sandwiches. She got out of the car and opened the front door cautiously, keen to avoid running into Holt, Poppy and Opal, but some bells attached to the door jangled. Inside was a cute café, with matching wooden furniture and a counter stacked with plates of cakes and cookies. But there were no staff around, and no customers either. She thought how lively the bar had been in comparison. Ragtown seemed far more of a beer drinkers' town. Behind the counter there was a handmade sign, inscribed with the words: *Any fool can know. The point is to understand.* An arrow beside it pointed toward a narrow spiral staircase. *Quirky.* If this was Florence's doing, she liked her already.

Savannah really wasn't a fan of perilous-looking staircases, but there didn't seem to be any other option, so she clung to the rail and negotiated the narrow stairs, trying hard to not look down.

When she reached the upper story, a cozy, homemade library was revealed, full of brightly colored chairs and beanbags, and bookshelves stuffed with books. The walls were decorated with more handmade signs, quirky quotes, and children's paintings and drawings. Garrett's children were sitting around a central table, opposite a curvy woman with red hair and glasses, who was showing them something from a large picture book.

Holt happened to look up from the desk, and immediately spotted her. "Savannah!" he exclaimed.

Reluctantly, she climbed up the two final steps and entered the room. Poppy and Opal jumped up and hugged her again, making sounds like tiny bear purrs.

"This is the lady who make the best cakes," Opal told the redhaired woman, who nodded and gave Savannah a peculiar look. It wasn't unfriendly, but it contained a mixture of curiosity and approval that she wasn't sure how to read.

"I'm Savannah," she said. "I'm new in town."

"And I'm Florence. It's a pleasure to meet you."

"I'm sorry for interrupting the lesson," Savannah said. "When would be a good time for me to come back and have a word with you?"

"Oh, the children were just about to take a very welcome break from their math lesson, so I'm free now." Florence beamed, as if she couldn't wait to chat. She directed the kids to go and play by the beanbags, and she turned her attention to Savannah.

"What can I do for you?" she said, smiling politely. She had an attractive, eager face, with round cheeks and somewhat mischievous eyes, behind a pair of red, '70s style glasses.

Savannah cleared her throat. "This is probably going to sound strange, but I got sent here by an agency called MateMatch, to meet the guy they'd matched me with. But it turns out they've made a mistake and he doesn't know anything about me or the agency, so I'm just trying to find them and sort this whole mess out."

Florence tented her fingers together. They were weighed down with a selection of large, quirky statement rings. "I see," she said slowly. "So, the agency sent you here? I'm sure they had a good reason for it."

Savannah shook her head. "No, I think the whole thing was a mistake. Maybe some kind of computer glitch or something."

Florence gave a bubbly laugh, making Savannah think of a naughty little chipmunk. "No one comes to Ragtown by mistake, my dear."

Savannah sighed. "But everyone I meet tells me I shouldn't be in Ragtown at all. That it's no place for humans."

Florence nodded solemnly. "You are likely the first human to move here, that's true. But I like to think that Ragtown has a place for everyone who needs it."

Do I need it? Savannah thought, discreetly running her eyes over Florence. If Florence was surviving here as a woman, maybe she could, too. But then, the thought of running into Garrett every day; wondering what might have been if he wasn't so opposed to taking her as his mate...

No, it could never work.

"The thing is, I need to find my real match, so I've got to speak to the agency," she said.

Florence shrugged her soft, round shoulders. "But perhaps it wasn't a mistake after all? It could be that your match didn't know he was matched with you?"

Savannah gaped. "Really?"

"Sometimes that's a method agencies employ, my dear." She gazed at Savannah expectantly, through thick lenses.

Savannah shook her head. "That's not for me. I'm not one to insist if I'm not wanted." She sighed. "I met the guy, and he told me straight out that he wasn't interested in having a mate." Another stab of rejection followed her words.

Florence's eyes filled with sympathy. "Well, I can't help with the agency, I'm afraid," she said slowly. "But it so happens that I'm looking for someone to work in the café, if you need a job while you're looking for your match."

"Y-you're offering me a job?" Savannah stuttered, so startled by the turn of events that her brain was struggling to catch up.

"Yes, my dear. You're probably thinking that the café is very empty." Florence gave her chipmunk laugh again. "But the people of this town need it. They don't know it yet, but I'm determined to convince them. I have a lot of plans, but so little time because I'm busy with school. You'd be doing me a big favor."

Savannah gazed around the cheerful, brightly-lit space, her thoughts whirling. *Stay in Ragtown?* The idea was strangely tempting. And there was no way she was going back to her old life. No way in hell. But she needed to find her mate, wherever he was. That was her priority.

"I'd like to help but I just don't know if I'm sticking around," she said.

Florence tilted her head to the side and batted her eyelashes. The effect wasn't very dramatic, because they were white-blonde and short, but Savannah appreciated the sentiment. "Aww, stay for a few days at least?" She leaned forward conspiratorially. "You see, I'm trying to put together a festival over the weekend, and I could definitely do with the help. Plus, a little bird has told me that you're talented at making cakes, and that would be a godsend for the café. Unfortunately, I wasn't blessed with baking talents. My cakes either end up like puffballs or frisbees."

Savannah pressed her lips together. She could do with the money, too, and something to distract her from her thoughts about Garrett while she figured out what had happened to her match gone-AWOL.

"Okay," she said slowly. "As long as you understand it's a short-term thing?"

Florence nodded eagerly. "Thank you my dear. I've got the feeling you won't regret it." She broke into a winning smile.

Savannah couldn't help liking her, although she got the distinct feeling that she was hiding something behind her cheerful exterior. "Oh—perhaps I should've mentioned—I have no idea how to use the coffee machine," she said.

Florence rubbed her hands together. "That's no problem at all. I can teach you, and you'll be knocking out cappuccinos and lattes before you know it." She turned around and looked for the kids who had abandoned the beanbag area, and were chasing each other up and down the room. "Okay, kids, we're going downstairs to teach Savannah how to make coffee."

Opal sprinted up to her and fixed Florence with her big, liquid eyes. "Can we have babyccinos?" she asked solemnly.

"If Savannah can make them for you!"

The spiral staircase looked hazardous for children, but the three of them turned around and clambered down it with ease. Shifter kids, Savannah reminded herself. Of course, they were going to be agile.

So, she was staying in Ragtown for a few more days. She turned over the thought as she descended the stairs much more cautiously, trying to ignore the vertigo that was making her head swim. But where on earth was she going to sleep? Garrett's place was not an option.

* * *

Garrett

GARRETT HAMMERED on the door of one of the more broken-down houses of Ragtown. "Tyrell, I know you're in there!" he roared. "I can smell your stinking hide from here."

Which was true. But inside was ominously silent. Half of the timber he'd sourced for the house he was renovating on the edge of town had disappeared during the night, and he was sure that waste-of-space wolf shifter, Tyrell, and his two sidekicks were behind it. Mostly because nobody else in the town would be so goddamn obvious. Not only that, but there was a huge pile of timber behind the house that looked very much like his.

"Tyrell! Don't make me come in and get you out!" He pounded on the door one final time.

As he took a step back and prepared to kick it in, it swung open, emitting a reek of unwashed bodies, followed by Tyrell's narrow snout and mean, yellow eyes. His dyed black hair was sticking up in greasy clumps.

Garrett wrinkled his nose deliberately. "You all have roaches in there, or you haven't showered in a month?" he demanded.

Tyrell narrowed his eyes. "What d'you want?"

Garrett stuck his hands in his pockets. "I want my timber back," he said calmly.

Tyrell raised both shoulders, which made him look more like a mutant rat than ever. "Don't know what you're talking about."

Garrett let off a patient sigh, belying the irritation that was bubbling up inside him. If he didn't get what he needed very soon, that wolf was going to be pinned against his doorpost by his throat. "I'm talking about the pile of timber behind your house which you and your buddies stole from me."

Tyrell bared his teeth. "That's our timber," he hissed.

His sidekicks, Dagger and Ransom, appeared behind him, peering over each of his shoulders. They were equally sleazy looking, also with badly-dyed black hair, but they were a heavier build, which explained why he'd picked them as his cohorts.

"You need to leave, bro," said one.

"Yeah, you do," grunted the other.

Garrett didn't know which was which; they were essentially interchangeable, with their big foreheads and weak chins. He let out a roar that made the three of them jump back in unison. "You keep squaring up to me like that and I'll grind you all to a pile," he growled. Fear showed in three sets of cunning eyes, and instinctively, their shoulders and haunches dropped in submission to the bigger shifter.

"I'm not leaving without my timber," he said through gritted teeth. "And you're going to pack it in my truck for me."

Tyrell gave a throaty snarl. "Give him the stupid timber," he muttered over his shoulder.

He turned his attention back to Garrett. "It's not yours. But since we need to live in this town, we'll play good neighbors." He spat on the dirt, an inch from Garrett's shoe.

Garrett let it ride. He folded his arms, and waited by his Ford pick-up while dumb and dumber carried the timber over, bickering with each other. He was doing his best to keep his cool, but he was furious that the wolves had moved to Ragtown. He knew they were up to something shady, and he wasn't looking forward to finding out what it was. Anyone was welcome to move to Ragtown. Shifters heard about it on the grapevine, through loose mouths or drunken chatter, and anyone desperate enough and determined enough could make a life for themselves up in this lonely mountain town. That was one of the things he liked about it—there weren't too many rules. Still, the more shifters who moved in, the more he thought there needed to be some kind of law office up here.

The wolves were taking their sweet time, and now he was late picking the kids up from school. His irritation increased. The children were his biggest priority, and he did his best to ensure that they never doubted that. "Hurry the hell up!" he bawled, his voice echoing in the quiet street. Dagger and Ransom jumped half out of their skins, then started to work double-time. But that wasn't saying a lot. With a groan, he pushed up his sleeves and went to join them.

When Garrett screeched up to the library in his truck, he was already running fifteen minutes late. Thankfully, Florence never gave him a hard time about it. He yanked the door open, burst into the room...and stopped dead.

Aidan, another of those runty-ass wolf shifters, was sitting at one of the tables in the café, while Savannah, dishcloth in hand, was standing six feet away from him, face stiff with shock and revulsion.

"... I'm a very passionate lover. And I've got a huge you-know-what," he was saying in his irritating voice.

Garrett's bear let out a savage roar and Aidan and Savannah jumped, their heads whipping toward him.

Aidan recovered fast, his face contorting into a stupid smirk. "Whoa! What's eating you?"

"Leave Savannah alone!" he barked.

The smirk stretched into a grin. "Why… are you jealous, big guy?"

Garrett clenched his fists and clamped his jaw shut, desperately trying to keep his bear in. It was scratching up his insides, bursting to tear Aidan apart. It took every ounce of his strength to hold back his shift. *Crap.* Why was it being so protective of Savannah?

"Savannah's taken," he snarled between his teeth.

Aidan kicked out a chair and put his foot up on it. "Hadn't realized congratulations were in order, bro," he drawled. He turned his head and looked at Savannah. "But I'd think again if I was you, doll," he told her. "I'll be a much better mate for you than this broken bear."

"I'm not Savannah's mate," Garrett roared.

"No?" Aidan laced his hands behind his head. "Then why is your bear popping out of you? Looks like it's about to rip a fit."

Garrett was one step away from ripping Aidan's smug face off, but seeing as his kids were upstairs, he chose to ignore him. Instead, he turned to Savannah. Her eyes were big and terrified, and he felt terrible. "What are you doing here?" he said in the softest voice he could muster.

She raised her hands and indicated the room. "Looks like I got a job here."

His bear purred. He coughed to conceal the sound. "You're sticking around, then?"

She twisted the dishrag between her hands. "I don't know yet. But Florence needs some help for the next few days at least."

He nodded, and because he couldn't stand the tension any longer, he took off for the library, racing up the ridiculously small staircase at full pelt. Holt, Opal and Poppy shrieked in excitement at the sight of him. He loved this part of each day. It made everything worthwhile—all the grief, the hard times, all the times he wondered if he'd ever be any good as a parent. The girls launched themselves at him and clambered all over him, using him as a makeshift climbing frame, while Holt rested his head against his ribcage, connecting with his bear. Garrett understood it was important for him to do that several times a day. He stroked his hair, thinking it was time they all got a cut. "Thanks, Florence," he mouthed over their heads.

"Anytime," Florence mouthed back and blew him a kiss.

He descended the stairs with difficulty, since Poppy insisted on sitting on his shoulders, while the other two went down backwards like the little bear cubs they were.

Savannah was still in the café, wiping down the tables. She kept her head down, but he could tell she was acutely aware of their presence, and his nostrils picked up the scent of her stress. He hated that he'd made her feel like that. He was hoping he could sneak out of the place without having to speak to her, when Opal yelled, "Savannah, are you making pizza for us again tonight?"

Garrett's stomach dropped like an elevator in freefall.

Savannah turned her head towards them, her cheeks flaming. It made her look extra pretty, he noticed distractedly. "Uh, no, not tonight, guys," she murmured.

"We're having barbecue tonight, kids," Garrett said quickly. Opal and Poppy made faces of boredom, while Holt whooped in delight. Being the oldest of the three, his bear was developing a stronger need for meat than the girls. Garrett thought about inviting Savannah to join them, but quickly decided against it. He didn't want to give her the wrong idea, and it wasn't good for his bear to be around her. The damn animal had been difficult to control ever since it first caught her scent, and it was only getting worse. He couldn't afford that kind of trouble.

"Okay, let's go," he said in a cheery voice and led his three charges to the exit. Halfway through the door, he stopped.

"Have you got a place to stay for the night?" he asked Savannah.

"Yes, I have," she said, making brief eye contact before dropping her head again. Her cheeks were still pink, poor thing. For one bad, wrong second, he imagined how she'd look lying beneath him in bed, her cheeks heated from arousal instead.

He tamped that thought right down. "That's good," he muttered and strode outside.

It was crazy how fast the kids had taken to Savannah, he thought as they piled into the open bed of the truck. They were good kids, but they didn't usually warm to people easily. It had taken them weeks to accept Florence when they first met her. He constantly felt guilty that he couldn't provide them with a mother. But he also couldn't trust himself to take a mate. He'd sworn to remain single for the rest of his life, and that was the only safe option for him… and every other female his bear liked.

CHAPTER 5

Florence was out of town for a couple of days, sourcing coffee beans for the weekend festival, and she'd left Savannah in charge of the café. It was quiet, shifters drifting in now and then, ordering coffees or sandwiches, and Savannah took advantage of all the free time to bake some cakes. The kitchen had a strange collection of utensils though, some of which looked like they'd been around since the Gold Rush, and it made her job a bigger challenge than she'd expected.

Florence was on a mission to stop the town's community from spending all their free time in the bar, and part of her strategy was to turn them into coffee drinkers instead. She handed out free samples and tried to educate them on the different types of beans, and her coffee festival was an attempt to bring it all out into the open, as she'd explained. Savannah liked the idea, but, judging by most of the inhabitants she'd met so far, it wasn't going to be an easy ride.

She was in the middle of mixing up the dough for a lemon cake when her phone's message alert pinged. She wiped her hands on her apron and checked it. It was from the matchmaking agency:

No, my dear, there's no mistake. Garrett, father to Opal, Poppy, and

Holt is your match. He's a wonderful shifter, and I believe you're very well-suited. Good luck!

"Good luck?" she muttered. She'd already explained to the pesky matchmaker that Garrett had denied signing up to the service, and told her that he wasn't looking for a mate. What part of that was so hard to understand? Really, they were unbelievable! She was now stuck in Ragtown because of their mistake, and they were refusing to take any responsibility. The pain of Garrett's rejection still burned inside her. She didn't blame him, though. She could see that he'd made a big sacrifice in looking after children that weren't his, and that some tragedy must have triggered it. And now this matchmaking agency had made things worse for both of them. She'd come here, resigned to mating without love, and instead she'd got yet more heartache. Sadness and anger heated her chest, and she fired off a reply to the agency:

Garrett is not my match. I don't know why you keep insisting he is. Where is your agency? I'm coming to speak to you in person!

She'd only just picked up the wooden spoon again when they replied:

I'm afraid we don't have a physical office, but you're welcome to share any queries you have via email.

She gave a yell of annoyance. *Queries?* Why on God's earth were they acting so stupid? She raised the phone up high, ready to hurl it at the nearest wall. She wasn't a violent person, but recent events had strained her almost to breaking point.

She dropped her hand again. Maybe it wasn't the agency playing dumb. Maybe somebody else was playing a trick on her. And the only person she could think of who'd do such a thing was Joel, her ex. He had a mean-streak a mile wide, and a passion for practical jokes.

She jabbed at her contacts button, located his entry and hit dial.

"Yeah, babe," he said in a sleepy, thick voice, as if she'd woken him. As if they'd last spoken half an hour earlier, and he hadn't dumped her and broken her heart several weeks ago.

"Are you trying to ruin my new life for me, Joel?" she yelled, skipping any pleasantries.

"Whuh?" he mumbled.

"I think you know exactly what I'm talking about! Someone's playing a trick on me, and you're the only asshole I know who'd be mean enough to do it!" Her voice was getting louder and louder, but since there were no customers present, she could shout as much as she liked.

"I don't know what you're talking about, hun. I haven't been playing any tricks on you…not since that time at your parents' anyway," he sniggered. He was referring to the time when he'd secretly tucked the back of her skirt into her panties when they were having dinner with her parents. Her cheeks heated with a fresh wave of embarrassment.

"Haven't you done enough already?" she demanded, not trusting his words one iota.

"I miss you," he butted in.

"What?" she muttered. Her eyes prickled, and she squeezed them shut. He'd dumped her and kicked her out of the house they shared because she couldn't have a baby. Nine months ago, a drunk driver had crossed on a red light and smashed into her car. It was a bad accident. She lost the baby she was carrying, and when the doctors told her that her womb was damaged and she wouldn't be able to have any more children, her wolf mate dumped her. Joel was the Alpha of his clan and a woman who couldn't conceive was no good to him. It had torn her heart in two, and all this time later, the pain was still fresh.

"I miss you," Joel repeated. "I made a mistake. My life's not the same without you. Come back to me, Sav."

A tear leaked from her eye and ran down her cheek as she relived that awful time again. "I can't have babies, Joel," she whispered into the phone.

"Doesn't matter. We can get a surrogate."

She drew in a ragged breath. Why hadn't he suggested that at the time? She'd pleaded with him to reconsider, to see if there were any other options, but he'd refused flat out. An Alpha's pups need to come from his mate's womb, he'd said. And that was that. That piece-of-shit drunk driver had ended her life as she knew it, and he'd got away with barely a scratch.

Could she go back to her life? Get in her car right now and drive all the way back to Wolf Creek and Joel, and the pack she missed? It would be so easy, such a comfort.

She wiped her eyes and cleared her throat.

"I haven't missed you one bit, Joel Carter," she said in a hard voice. "I'm better off without you and your selfish ways."

"I'm sorry, Savannah. I wish I could take it all back—" he began.

"You should've thought about all that before you showed me the door. I pleaded with you, tried to reason with you, but you treated me like everything we'd had meant nothing to you. I never want to see you as long as I live. Stop screwing up my new life by playing mean jokes on me!" She jabbed the end-call button and stuffed her phone in her back pocket.

Tears coursed down her face, but she chose to ignore them as she returned to stirring the cake mix. She hoped desperately that would be the end of it. And she was going to drop the whole matchmaking thing. It had been a big mistake, but she'd been through worse and survived. She'd stay in Ragtown a few more days, until she'd figured out a new plan for her life, then she'd be on her way.

TWO HOURS LATER, four perfectly-cooked cakes were sitting on the counter, making Savannah's mouth water. Somehow, angry mixing had turned out a very light, fluffy dough. There was an orange cake, a lemon cake, a double chocolate cake and a carrot cake. She cut some slices from each, and laid them on a big wooden tray, and she poured some freshly brewed coffee into small, disposable cups and put them on the tray, too, then she carried everything out of the café and went out onto Main Street.

Florence had told her that as long as she was carrying goodies, she wouldn't have issues with the locals, but still her stomach tightened in apprehension. She'd spent the last two nights at Florence's place, always by her side, and there had been no need for her to venture out alone. It was late afternoon—around the same time that of day she'd arrived in Ragtown three days earlier— but at least the semi-deserted streets were starting to feel familiar. She walked slowly down the dirt road, calling out, "free coffee and cake!" as Florence had suggested.

Soon, heads started poking out of doors, then a stream of shifters scurried over and snatched at the cake. Most of them communicated with no more than a grunt, but a few of them said it was very tasty. The coffee was a harder sell, and she only managed to get rid of three cups, despite her best attempts to convince the shifters that it was delicious. There were no women, not a single one. Florence had explained that living in isolation was more of a guy-thing, and the feral feel of the place tended to put women off. So far, she'd been very vague about what she was doing in Ragtown, and Savannah imagined it would take a lot of probing to get to the truth. Hell, she'd probably be long gone before that happened.

When she returned to the café, a big, stocky guy was peering through the window.

"Hey there," she called in a friendly voice, but he jumped guiltily.

"Just wondering if the library is open," he muttered in a deep, slow voice. He had different colored eyes, and she remembered he was the guy who'd snarled at her and given her a warning look when she'd first walked into the bar. He was a bear shifter, she deduced. She was getting good at this now. Before she'd arrived here, the only shifters she'd ever known were wolves. But now she knew that bears were huge and intimidating, but generally had kind eyes, and a big, sexy handsomeness. Like Garrett, she thought, and her stupid heart twinged again.

Was it a good idea to let him upstairs? He seemed withdrawn, but less hostile than most of the guys she'd met.

"Don't want to bother you," he continued haltingly.

"Florence is away, but you can go in," she said at last. She wasn't sure how the lending process worked, but she'd just make a note of which books he took, and tell Florence later, she decided.

He nodded. "Appreciate that."

She showed him inside, and he insisted on helping her with the tray she was carrying.

"Can I interest you in some coffee and cake?" she asked.

To her surprise, he tried a slice of both orange and lemon cake, and washed them down with not one, but two coffees. "These are really good," he said. "Compliments to the chef."

She couldn't help blushing. "I'll pass them on," she said and they both laughed. He looked different when he laughed, less edgy and hunted. She showed him the stairs to the library, and he just managed to squeeze his bulk up the spiral staircase. He headed to the bookshelves eagerly.

"I'll be downstairs. Just holler if you need anything," she told him.

As she walked down the first couple of steps, clinging tight to the rail, the café door banged open and several people charged in. Her heartbeat sped up.

When she saw it was Garrett and the children, relief rolled through her, swiftly followed by a jab of adrenaline.

Garrett looked worried, his dark eyes blazing. "Is Florence back yet?" he said with no preamble.

"I'm not expecting her until later in the evening," she told him. The children rushed to her and she hugged them all as best she could.

Garrett's face tensed even more, the muscles in his broad jaw flexing. "Sorry to ask, but would you mind watching the kids for a few hours? There's been an accident at the mine."

"An accident?" she echoed.

"A ramp collapsed, and the mine owner's stuck down there. We've got to get him out."

"Oh my God. Is he hurt?"

"We don't know yet." His eyes were full of panic.

Of course, I'll look after the children, for as long as you need. Just go."

"Thank you." He flashed a look of gratitude. "Be good, kids, okay?" he said to them.

"I hope everything's okay. And—be careful," she called, as he dashed from the room.

* * *

Garrett

THE COLLAPSE HAD BURIED Brock under a pile of earth. At first, he'd responded to their shouts, but now he was silent, and Garrett's panic increased by the second. He, Jagger and Callan had scrabbled down the mine shaft and they were digging with spades as fast as they could, desperate to reach him.

Many minutes passed. It was tough going, and Garrett's muscles burned from the exertion, while sweat poured down his face. They kept yelling his name, listening in vain for his response.

At long last, they uncovered the base of the ramp and, lying with his head beneath it in what seemed like an air pocket, was Brock. But he was unconscious. Garrett's gut clenched. Had he run out of air? In a frenzy, he grabbed the big shifter and shook him.

Brock groaned.

Then he gasped and sucked in a huge lungful of air. Everyone laughed in relief.

"Thought you were a goner, big guy," Jagger said.

Brock gave a dry laugh that turned into a hacking cough. "Guess I would've been if you guys hadn't come to find me."

"Let's get you out of here," Garrett said. "Are you hurt?"

Brock moved his limbs, testing them. "Don't think so." A pile of earth was still covering his legs, and he fought to free them. When the others helped him to stand up, more earth started to fall down from above.

"Shit." Shielding his eyes, Garrett looked up. "I think the whole tunnel's going to collapse. Come on!"

Getting out was a lot harder than going in. The tunnel was on a steep slant and, without the ramp, it was an impossible task. Clods of earth kept falling down, and Garrett's panic grew.

"Come on," he muttered to his bear. Immediately, it rose to the surface. *Riiiip!* went his shirt and jeans, and it burst out of him. Jagger's bear was quick to follow, while Brock took on his lion form.

"Stand back," Callan muttered, a moment before his dragon burst out of him, scales glimmering in the darkness and dark green wings sprouting from his back. With his talons, he reached for Brock and Jagger, and Garrett dug his claws into Jagger's thick hide, and they scrabbled their way out of the mine shaft.

Callan hauled them out into the daylight and they collapsed on the ground, all panting and gasping for air.

Garrett shook his head. That had been a close one. Too close for comfort. That damned mine. It seemed to bring nothing but trouble. He got to his feet, preparing to shift back, but there was a wild roar behind him, and before he could turn, two sets of razor-sharp talons dug into his shoulders. Instinctively, he threw his weight backward and crashed to the ground, pinning his attacker beneath him. He rolled over to discover it was Brock, his eyes red and rolling, foam spewing from his mouth. His fucking beast was out of control. It had turned feral, and when it got like that, it felt no pain, and it took the strength of at least two shifters to subdue it.

Brock clawed at his face, ripping his flesh. Garrett yelled out in pain, and slashed at Brock's muzzle. Brock shook his head, throwing out a spray of blood, but it barely slowed him down, and he was back again, attacking to kill.

Jagger rushed to Garrett's aid, and they fought to crush the beast, pressing it with their weight, trying to cut off its air supply. Brock was getting cut up plenty, but he wouldn't quit, and he lashed out again and again with his big-cat claws, while his huge jaws bit through bear hide with ease. Garrett didn't want to put him down, but it was fast getting to that point, with he and Jagger getting more and more torn up, the metallic tang of blood thick in the air.

Suddenly, a dark shape blocked out the sun. There was a whoosh and a jet of flame, and Brock howled and rolled away from them.

Smoke and the reek of burning flesh choked Garrett's nostrils, and Callan hung over them, leathery wings flapping. Garrett hunkered down, breathing hard and assessing the damage. Jagger's thick hide had some open gashes, while Brock was more blood than fur and his tail had been burned by a jet of Callan's fire breath. That furry tuft at the end, that all lion shifters were so damn proud of was gone. As Garrett regained his human shape, his skin burned all over from his injuries.

"Shift!" he bawled at Brock.

Brock took on his human shape and the madness receded from his eyes. He gasped in pain at his injuries. "I'm sorry," he panted, hanging his head in shame.

Garrett ground his teeth and glared at him. Brock knew his beast got crazy like that. That was why he'd moved to Ragtown after all, to keep himself out of harm's way. He loathed the feral side of himself, and avoided shifting under any circumstances. But he'd lost it and almost killed them all.

Garrett longed to bawl him out; tear him a new one. But Brock needed help, not punishment. He got that.

Callan hovered overhead, no doubt worried they hadn't seen the last of Brock's beast. But when Brock continued to cower, his lower back horribly burned from where his tail had been scorched, Callan dropped back to earth and folded his wings back into his body, then his shimmering, dark-green scales and long, dragon snout receded.

He stalked up to Brock, fists bunched. "What the fuck?" he roared. "We risk our asses trying to save yours, and then you try to take us out? This is how you repay us?"

Brock's head dropped even lower. "I'm sorry. My beast. It was all the adrenaline. Turned it crazy."

Callan shook his head hard. "You shouldn't have shifted. I could've carried you out as a human. Would've been easier actually. That miserable lion of yours didn't help me any."

Brock's head snapped up, his lion's arrogance breaking through. "Didn't ask you to help me," he snarled. "You should've just let me die in there." He got to his feet and stormed off.

"Wish I had—" Callan roared, but Garrett caught his arm.

"Let him go," he said. "He's embarrassed. I know he's grateful for what we did, but now he's eaten up with shame. He's got some serious issues, but—"

"He needs putting down," Callan snapped, amber eyes blazing. "Too many issues, even for Ragtown."

"No such thing," Jagger muttered grimly. "If we haven't got a chance up here, what have we got?"

"He's right," Garrett said. "Let's give him one more chance."

Callan snorted, and smoke poured from his nostrils. Then, without another word, he turned and stalked off down the road, buck naked.

Garrett glanced down at his bloodied flesh in dismay. "Another shirt, jeans, underwear and boots gone," he muttered to Jagger, who grunted in agreement. He didn't have a lot of clothes to start with. He ought to send Brock the bill. As if that damn lion had any money to speak of, he thought, with a grim laugh.

He needed to get himself home and get cleaned up. He was just glad that the kids were safe in the library with Savannah. He'd hate for any of them to see him like that.

* * *

It was dark and way past the children's bedtime by the time Garrett got back to pick them up. They weren't in the café, but he could hear Savannah's voice filtering down from the library, and a stab of guilt went through him. He went upstairs, climbing the narrow metal treads on quiet feet. She was sitting on a beanbag reading from a children's book, while Holt, Poppy and Opal were curled up on beanbags in front of her, more asleep than not. There was a soft glow in the room, and it looked peaceful and homely. There was a tiny flicker in his chest, like a flame beginning to catch.

When Savannah caught sight of him, her eyes went wide, and she gasped. Of course. He looked a state. His right eyebrow was bust open, it felt like there was a bunch of claw marks running down his left cheek, and his forearms were covered in wounds.

He went over to her and bent to her ear. "I'm okay," he murmured. "And so's Brock. We all got out unscathed." Her sweet, feminine scent filled his nostrils, and his loins stirred. *Crap.* It was a bad idea to get so close to her.

"And this?" She pointed a trembling finger at his arm.

"Collateral damage," he said and gave her what was supposed to be a playful smile. Carefully, so as not to wake the children, she started to get up. But she was struggling to push herself up from the squishy beanbag, and he stretched out his hands to help her. To his surprise, she slid her hands into his. Her fingers were wonderfully slender, and her palms soft. He hadn't expected physical contact between them to feel so intense, and he almost let go in shock. She looked up at him, her pupils huge. "Come with me," she whispered.

Dumbly, he followed her down the staircase and into the café.

"I'm going to clean your wounds," she announced, disappearing behind the counter.

"No, that's not necessary."

She spun around. "Garrett, have you seen yourself? You're all cut up." As she scanned his injuries, her lower lip trembled, and suddenly her eyes got very bright.

She cared, and it wrenched at him. "I'm a shifter. Our wounds heal fast," he said gruffly.

She blinked fast, as if trying to dismiss her emotions, then made a clicking sound with her tongue. She took a first aid box out of a cupboard and instructed him to sit down on one of the chairs. "Let me take a look."

Capable as well as feisty, he thought. He liked this side of her. But when she laid her soft fingertips on his skin, he tingled all over.

It was as if she had electricity running through her veins. She made soft, sympathetic sounds as she swabbed at his many cuts and gashes with some kind of antiseptic solution.

He wasn't used to being cared for like this, and he was surprised to find that he was enjoying it. From time to time, her long hair brushed his face, and he picked up her intimate, floral scent. It reminded him of the honeysuckle that used to grow in his yard when he was a child. He had a crazy urge to pull her onto his lap and cover her in kisses.

"What happened?" she murmured.

He hesitated. Shifters didn't discuss their nature with humans. But here she was, in a shifter town, because she wanted to get mated to a shifter. "We managed to pull Brock out of the mine—just in time, as more of it started to collapse—but we all had to shift to get out, and Brock went a little crazy."

She gasped. "He attacked you when you were rescuing him?"

When he lifted his head, she was gazing at him intently, her eyes the deep blue of a stormy sea.

"I know it sounds bad. But he couldn't help it. He's got some of the shifter madness, and he turns feral when his adrenaline is high."

"Madness," she breathed. "Isn't it dangerous having him in Ragtown?"

"Ragtown is dangerous. Brock isn't the most screwed up shifter here. Not by a long shot. Everyone who lives here has problems that make them unfit for mainstream society." He held her gaze, looking at her seriously. "It's important you understand that if you want to stay here, Savannah. Blood gets shed every single day in Ragtown. Make no mistake about that. That's why you shouldn't be out alone at night."

"I get that," she said in a quiet voice, but a question seemed to hang on her lips. He sensed she was wondering what his screwup was. But he wasn't about to share that with her.

"And you still want to stay here?" he said.

"I do. The matchmaking agency warned me that Ragtown is like no other place in the country, maybe in the whole world, and that I need to keep my wits about me." She shrugged. "But I thought it was worth a chance."

He frowned. Was that because the fake profile they'd sent her made him sound like such a nice guy? Suddenly, his protective instinct rose up. He wanted to tell her that he'd be with her always, and no one would ever hurt her again.

But that was ridiculous. He was the last guy who was in a position to do that.

Savannah was quiet for a while. "Okay, all done," she said at last, surveying her work. He stunk like a pharmacy, but he'd enjoyed her attentions, her caring, gentle touches.

"Thanks."

"No problem. I'm glad the kids were sleeping when you arrived—they would've been shocked to see you in that state."

"You're right. I just felt so bad about leaving them with you for so long that I rushed back as soon as I could. Thanks again for taking care of them."

"You didn't have to rush back. It was my pleasure. They're such great kids."

He could tell from her eyes that she meant it, and he got to his feet slowly, an idea forming itself in his mind. He could really do with some help with the children. His planned renovations on the house had barely progressed during the last few months, and he'd also promised Jagger that he'd help with the sheriff's office he was trying to set up. Florence was a great help with the school, but he knew he was monopolizing her time.

"What is it?" Savannah asked, looking at him very curiously.

"What's what?"

"The question on your mind." Her eyes were full of light and understanding, as if they were looking right into his soul, and he startled. How did she know that? Women seemed to have a way of knowing you better than you knew yourself. Maybe that was why this was a bad idea.

"I was wondering if you might be interested in being a nanny to

Holt, Opal and Poppy. The offer comes with the bed in the spare room, too," he blurted out.

Savannah's mouth opened and closed again, revealing the tip of her pink tongue. He'd taken her by surprise. Did she think he was being inappropriate? That wasn't it. Definitely not.

"I mean, the bed offer is, uh, for convenience," he stuttered.

Savannah blinked several times, her long eyelashes fluttering. *Shit*, that seemed to have made things even more awkward.

"Can I think about it?" she said at last.

"Sure." He let out a long breath of relief. "You know where to find me," he added in what he hoped was a jokey tone.

CHAPTER 6

The next morning, Savannah was in the café, leafing through a cookbook. Timon was sitting in the far corner, drinking a cup of coffee and reading a book. He didn't say much, but she liked having him there. He was a comforting presence, somehow.

She was looking for some new recipes to try, but her thoughts kept turning to Garrett's offer. She was very unsure about the whole thing. If she accepted, she definitely couldn't leave Ragtown any time soon. It wouldn't be good for the children. Having obviously lost their parents, what they needed most was stability in life, and she couldn't let them down.

And there was that other thing—her ridiculous attraction to Garrett, which only seemed to grow stronger by the day. Yesterday, the moment she'd laid her hands on his poor arm, she regretted offering to clean up his wounds. Being so close to him like that had been unbearable. She'd started tingling all over, and such heat had flooded through her that she was surprised he hadn't felt it. Living in the same house as him, feeling like that, would be awful. Deliberately or not, the guy was messing with her head, and was clearly very unavailable. She didn't know how her heart would cope.

The door swung open, and Florence bustled in. She was wearing a pretty, floral dress, her red hair flying everywhere. "You're a genius!" she exclaimed, hurrying to the counter.

"I am?" Savannah said, suppressing a smile of amusement.

"Your cakes have worked magic, my dear! Several people in town have asked me where they can get some more. This may be just what we need to get everyone coming to the café!"

Savannah beamed. "I'm so glad. I do enjoy making cakes, and I've got a ton of ideas."

"Wait here," Florence instructed, heading off to the staircase. She hurtled upstairs and was back a moment later with an armful of cookbooks. She spread them out on the counter and leafed through them eagerly, saying "how about this one? Or this? Or this?"

Savannah smiled at her indulgently, appreciating her energy.

Suddenly, Florence went very still, and stared at her owlishly. "I've had a great idea! What d'you think about becoming a business partner in the café?"

Now it was Savannah's turn to freeze. Two job offers in twenty-four hours? It was more than her brain could process. If she accepted Florence's offer, she'd have to say no to Garrett. But was that even a good idea?

Florence's face fell. "You hate the idea, don't you? I've put too much pressure on you."

"No, no, it's not that." Savannah let out a long breath. "Garrett has offered me the nanny job, complete with the spare room in his house. I mean, the kids are great. I really like them. And I can see that Garrett also needs the help. Plus, taking care of Garrett's children might be my only chance at motherhood."

Florence raised an eyebrow, and Savannah's cheeks flamed. *Crap.* She hadn't intended to blurt that out. Luckily, Florence was too discreet to ask her what she meant.

"Well, I think that's a great opportunity. You should definitely go for it," Florence said, clasping her hands excitedly, her garish rings flashing in the light. "I think it'll work out really well for all of you."

Savannah looked at Florence curiously, thinking that she seemed a little too excited about the idea, and she had no idea why.

"But regardless of what you decide, my offer of business partnership still stands," Florence continued.

Savannah frowned. "Are you sure? Because, if I become the kids' nanny, I won't be able to work full-time in the café."

"That's fine, my dear." Florence patted her arm. "As long as you bring your cake-baking skills to the table, I'm sure we can work something out."

* * *

AFTER WORK, Savannah drove to Garrett's house. She parked up and knocked on the door. And knocked again. She could hear banging, but there was no answer. She knocked one final time, waited thirty more seconds, then turned around to leave.

When she reached her car, Garrett appeared from the side of the house. His mouth was set in a hard line and his eyes were blazing. Adrenaline flickered inside her, but his expression softened a little when he saw her. His hands were covered in oil, and so was his chest, which was fully exposed to her gaze. She tried hard not to goggle at his huge pecs and perfectly honed abs, but the sight of them was doing things to her that she didn't want to acknowledge.

"Is this a bad time?" she asked.

He rubbed the back of his hand across his forehead. "What do you need?"

Savannah swallowed. This wasn't how she'd imagined the conversation going. "I've had time to think about your offer, and I've decided to accept," she said. But as the words left her mouth, she regretted them.

"Good," he said. Then he turned and walked back towards the rear of the house. She stood and watched him, nonplussed.

Then she shook herself. "Uh, excuse me? Aren't you going to show me around or something?" she called.

He glanced at her over his shoulder, his eyes quizzical. "You've been here before, what's there to show?"

Savannah's anger flared. "You know, you're making the prospect of working for you seem real attractive!"

Garrett turned to face her, and his expression shifted. "I'm sorry." He sighed. "My truck broke down and I've been struggling with it all afternoon."

"I'm sorry. But you definitely can't treat me like that if I work for you."

His eyes darkened with guilt. "I won't. I'm truly sorry, Savannah."

She folded her arms and regarded him, lips pursed. She had the sense he was the type of person who didn't apologize easily.

"Okay, you're forgiven," she said at last. She'd let him off the hook this one time.

He broke into a smile that lit up his whole face. To her annoyance, her heart fluttered. When his attention was on her, she felt special, like she was the only one who existed for him. What a ridiculous thought. She blushed at her own silliness.

He washed his hands in a sink at the side of the building. "I'll give you the tour now," he said.

She allowed herself to gaze at his broad back as he led her into the house. Muscles bunched and flexed at every little movement of his body. She watched, mesmerized as he lifted an arm to scratch the back of his neck, and the big muscles behind his shoulder went into a symphony of activity. A rivulet of perspiration ran down the sexy valley in the middle of his back. For one stupid moment, she thought about catching it with her tongue.

He showed her into the kitchen first, where there was a mess of flour on the table. "Dammit," he muttered, swiping at the back of his neck again. "I forgot about that. I was trying to make pancakes this morning, and that's what happened."

She burst out laughing, and he joined in.

"I was wondering what that was on your cheek," she said. Impulsively, she stepped closer to him and brushed a dab of flour off his cheek, just where his stubble began. It was a gentle gesture, but when she met his eyes, there was that feral look in them again. She shouldn't have done that. The tension between them was so strong, and standing so close to him was lighting her body on fire. Her nose picked up the scent of his fresh perspiration and the clean smell of his skin, and she longed for him to take her in his arms and crush her body against his, oil and grease and all. He stood very still, his lips inches from hers. Her heart beat fast.

Abruptly, he moved away. "I'll show you the bedrooms," he said.

Disappointment crashing through her, she followed him into the hallway.

He opened the door of the kids' room first. The window was small, as were all the windows in the house, but the walls were brightly decorated with murals of happily grinning animals. "Mainly Holt's handiwork," he explained. There were two beds on opposite sides of the room, and one in the middle.

"Who sleeps where?" she asked.

"Officially, that's Holt's, Opal's, Poppy's," he pointed them out. "But the girls are pretty interchangeable. Most nights they end up sharing a bed."

"Aw, that's so sweet." She took in the cartoon-themed comforters, and all the toys lying around the room, and she was amazed that Garrett had managed to bring so much civilization up to Ragtown.

Next, he showed her the spare bedroom, which she was already acquainted with. And, finally, his own bedroom. Her heartbeat sped up again as he swung the door open. It felt very intimate seeing his private lair, the bed where he slept every night. She tried her best not to imagine lying down on it with him, him stripping her naked, his hands running all over her bare body...

"Are you okay?" Garrett's tone was quizzical.

Damn, she'd been daydreaming about having sex with him while he was standing right beside her. *What was wrong with her?*

"Yeah I'm fine. Just a little tired I guess." She dragged her gaze away from the big bed with its plain gray comforter. The room was all plain and functional. A typical guy's room, but it smelled clean, and it was imbued with his musky, woodsy scent. "You have a lovely home," she said. "And I love that it's by the river."

"Being near water relaxes me," he said.

"Me too," she replied, and their eyes met again with that uncomfortable electricity.

"Where are the children?" she demanded, eager to break the tension.

"With my friend, Jagger." He led her out of the bedroom and closed the door firmly, as if also grateful to be escaping the intimacy of the space.

"Oh, I've met Jagger. He got rid of Aidan when he was bothering me one morning."

Garrett nodded. "Jagger's like that. He's a good guy. And Aidan's basically harmless, annoying though he is."

She smiled. "He's nothing I can't handle."

"The kids get passed around town like that when I'm working," he explained.

She raised an eyebrow. "From what I've seen so far, this town seems to be full of paternal shifters," she joked, then wondered if he'd take offense.

But he laughed loudly. "When I say *passed around*, I mean to the small number of people that I'd trust with my life."

Savannah nodded in sympathy. Raising three kids alone obviously stretched him to his limit. She still had a nagging doubt that she'd made the wrong decision to be the children's nanny. Garrett was obviously very casual about walking around shirtless, with apparently no idea how sexy he was. And she had a feeling that seeing him every day was going to do all kinds of things to her hormones and heart. But he and the children needed her, and that was what mattered.

CHAPTER 7

What on earth had he been thinking by asking Savannah to be the children's nanny? Garrett wondered the following afternoon, leaning against the kitchen counter and watching her chatting with the kids at the table. It had been less than a day, and he already couldn't get her out of his head. He was constantly restless around her, his bear tearing him up inside, insisting she was his mate. Those curves. That smile. Those fiercely intelligent blue eyes. And that sassy personality. He was starting to understand that she wouldn't put up with anyone's shit in Ragtown—least of all his. She was so great with the kids, too, instinctively knowing how to keep them entertained, and treating them like she loved them, even though they barely knew each other. His chest warmed every time he saw her interacting with them. Just as it was doing now. Dammit. He had to get out of there. Muttering that he'd be back soon, he stormed out of the kitchen and through the front door.

And almost collided with Jagger.

Jagger threw his hands up. "Woah! Why so worked up? Where's the fire?"

"I'm fine," he snapped.

Jagger gave him one of his tolerant looks. He was used to Garrett's outbursts of temper, and took them in his stride. "Who's the female inside the house?" he asked.

"Got myself a nanny," Garrett said shortly.

Jagger chuckled. "Is that what you call it?"

Garrett growled at him, but Jagger just laughed louder.

"I was hoping I could speak to you," he said. "I'm thinking I need a deputy in the sheriff's office. Those stinking wolves are causing more and more havoc through the town, and Florence's coffee festival thing is coming up. I could do with an extra pair of hands."

Garrett sighed. "You know they stole all my timber the other day? I had to go and threaten them before I got it back. I've also got a feeling my truck breaking down was no accident. I think they screwed with the engine."

Jagger's heavy brow furrowed. "Wouldn't put it past them. Any more crap out of any of them and they're outta here."

"What about Aidan for deputy? He looks like he's in need of gainful employment. And since he's a wolf, he might be better at dealing with them than we are."

Jagger shook his head. "Aidan's a troublemaker."

"He is, and that's why he needs something to keep him busy."

Jagger snorted. "I'm trying to run a sheriff's office, not a kindergarten. I was thinking of Ryker."

Garrett shook his head slowly. "Ryker's got serious anger issues. Plus, isn't he busy delivering stuff around town all day?"

"He can do both. And that's what makes him a good candidate. While he's making deliveries, he can keep an eye out for anything suspicious. Catch people off-guard."

Garrett sighed. "I'm just worried he'll end up killing someone. You know he's got a short fuse. Someone rubs him up the wrong way, that could be it."

The door opened and Savannah appeared. Garrett's chest gave an automatic jolt at the sight of her.

"Hey, Jagger. Good to see you again," she said with a smile.

Garrett's bear snarled, and he coughed in an effort to hide it. It didn't like the way she was smiling at Jagger. But what the hell? Was he jealous now?

"Heard you're sticking around for a while?" Jagger said conversationally.

She glanced at Garrett, and stupidly, his heart warmed. "Looks that way. I'm going to be working as nanny to Holt, Opal and Poppy. At least for a while."

"I'm sure you'll be very happy here. They're great kids. And Garrett's okay, when he's not like a bear with a sore head, anyway."

Garrett snarled, but Jagger slapped him on the shoulder playfully.

"I can get a bit like that myself, sometimes," said Savannah. "Think I'm equal to handling a grumpy bear."

"She's tough," Garrett said, and he couldn't keep the admiration out of his voice. Jagger slid him a significant look, which he chose to ignore.

"The kids tell me there's a park around the corner," Savannah said. "I was planning to take them now. You guys want to join us?"

The thought of watching Savannah running around, playing with the kids was appealing. Too appealing. What he actually needed was some time away from her so he could get his bear under control again. Convince it that nothing was going to happen between them.

"No, I can't. I'm busy with Jagger," he said.

Jagger raised his hands and dropped them again. "I think we're done here. I got the advice I needed. You should go," he told Garrett. There was a conspiratorial expression in his eyes that Garrett did not understand or appreciate.

Garrett tossed him a hostile look. "Okay, I'll join you," he mumbled to Savannah.

"Great!" she beamed at him, and his heart did that silly lifting thing again, making him feel like he was in a fast-ascending elevator. Then she turned to Jagger. "You want to come, too?"

Garrett's bear scrabbled inside him, urging him to make a claim on her. He clenched his jaw and pushed it back down, deep inside him.

"I can't," Jagger said quickly, as if he'd sensed Garrett's bear. "I have to go speak to Ryker, actually. Catch you guys later." And with that, he was off.

Garrett's jealousy dissipated, swiftly replaced by shame. He couldn't believe his bear was acting like that around Savannah, and that it was threatening to challenge Jagger. He shouldn't be thinking about Savannah that way at all, especially since she was a human. He was too screwed up for her. For anyone.

* * *

Savannah

"Let's walk along the river!" Holt demanded.

"It's a nice route," Garrett muttered to Savannah, but he looked away from her as if he didn't want to be out walking with her at all.

They passed through the yard and joined the river at the back of the house. Opal clambered up Garrett's leg, and he lifted her up and put her on his shoulders. Savannah marveled at her agility, thinking that a human child wouldn't be able to do that. She often forgot the kids were little shifters, and she had to catch herself when she saw them exhibiting unusual feats of strength. Poppy started clambering up her leg, too, but Garrett stopped her.

"Take it easy, Squirt," he said, tousling the little girl's hair. "Savannah is not a shifter, and her shoulders weren't designed for carrying little bear cubs around."

The kids gazed at her, stunned.

Poppy stopped dead in front of her. "Then what are you?" she demanded, mouth gaping open.

Savannah laughed. "I'm a human."

"You don't have an animal?" Holt said.

"Nope." Savannah indicated her body. "I'm just like this, one-hundred percent of the time."

The children regarded her with a mixture of curiosity and pity. "Wow," they said, echoing each other.

"There are plenty of other humans in the world," Garrett said. "But you'll learn more about that when you grow up."

It *was* lovely walking along the river, the water tinkling and gurgling beside them as it ran over the pebbly river bed, and a light, sweet breeze blowing. But after the conversation about humans, Garrett fell into a grumpy silence. Savannah tried to ignore it, focusing her attention on the kids instead, who had insisted on removing their shoes and running directly through the river, but doubts about being their nanny rose up in her mind again. She caught him up.

"Florence has asked me to be her business partner in the café," she began.

"That's great," he said, brightening instantly.

"But I've been wondering if I can combine it with being the kids' nanny."

He nodded thoughtfully. "See how it goes, but if you need to quit your job with us, then I understand."

What? Rejection pierced her. She'd been working for him for less than a day, and he was already so eager to get rid of her. Why did he even bother asking her to be the nanny? Her eyes pricked with tears. She blinked them away angrily. He was a complicated bear. And she hadn't begun to get to know him. She'd take his advice though: see how it went for a couple more days, then make a decision.

She moved away from him and focused her attention on the children instead. All three of them were now drenched from head to foot, but Garrett didn't seem to mind, and they were laughing and having a lot of fun, skimming stones and trying to catch fish with their bare hands. Their antics made her smile, but something dark and hollow continued to tug at her heart. And the longer they walked, the more her thoughts spiraled out of control. She'd always wanted a family like this—minus the grumpy bear. That was what she'd been hoping to find when she came to Ragtown, but all she'd found was more disappointment and rejection. Garrett didn't really want her around. Maybe he thought he was helping her out by offering her the job. She was just a charity case to him. Maybe Florence thought the same. What was she doing staying in this rough town where it wasn't even safe to walk around by herself? There were so many other places where she'd have a better chance of finding a mate. Where she wouldn't have to see Garrett every day.

"Are you okay?" Garrett asked.

"I'm fine," she said more curtly than she'd intended.

He nodded and kept going. At last, a scrubby patch of grass appeared alongside the river.

"The park!" Opal exclaimed, and she, Poppy and Holt sprinted over to it, and started chasing each other around.

"It's as much of a park as we get up here." Garrett threw Savannah an apologetic glance.

"It's… nice," she said hesitantly. The ground was lumpy, and the grass was long and choked with weeds. A lone tree stood in the middle, so ancient and spindly that it looked like a good gust of wind could take it down.

"Fixing it up is a project for the future. When I get some free time," Garrett said.

Out of nowhere, a familiar melody started up. It was so out of place in Ragtown that it took her a minute to identify it as the sound of an old-fashioned ice-cream truck. She looked around curiously. The only vehicle in sight was a beat-up pickup truck, and the music seemed to be coming out of the window.

"That's weird," she muttered, but the kids rushed to Garrett and bounced around him.

"Can we?" Holt pleaded, while the girls shrieked and whined.

"Okay, but just a small cone each," he told them.

"It's Ryker's truck," he said, turning to Savannah. "Sometimes he sells ice cream out the back of it. It's a very rare treat."

Just then his phone rang. "Oh, I need to get this."

"I'll take them if you like?" Savannah offered.

"Thanks." He flashed her a smile and answered the call.

"Let's go, kids," she said, and two small hands slid into hers.

A man was squatting in the flat bed of the truck, behind a cooler containing four ice cream tubs. He had a narrow face, and a lean, hungry look. Big-cat shifter, Savannah thought as his narrow green eyes met hers. He seemed unkempt, in a dangerous way, with his scruffy beard and ragged T-shirt, but the kids weren't afraid of him.

He shot them all a hostile look. "What are you having?" he said gruffly as they approached.

"What have you got?" Savannah countered, planting a hand on her hip. She was fast learning that the way to deal with the men of Ragtown was by facing them down and giving as good as she got.

"Vanilla bean, cookie dough, pistachio, and strawberry." He jabbed at each tub with a scoop, as violently as if it was a weapon. She asked the kids what they were having, and they picked two flavors each, and she picked pistachio. She was looking in her purse for some coins, when her nostrils wrinkled at the sudden arrival of a sour, oniony odor, and a mean voice said, "well, look-ee what we've got here."

She whirled around and came face to face with three smirking men. They had greasy hair, dirty clothes, and they all stank. *Wolf.* She swallowed hard. She'd met many mean-spirited wolves in her time. Some were kindhearted, but when they were bad, they were some of the worst.

"What brings you to Ragtown, little missy?" one of them demanded in a nasal voice.

"What's your name, honeybun?" demanded another.

She inserted herself in front of the children, using her hands to gather them behind her. "That's none of your business," she said, her calm tone belying the tension darting through her.

The one who'd spoken first raised an eyebrow. "I think this dull town just got a little better, what you think, boys? We've been looking for a sweet piece of ass to share between us." He cackled nastily.

"Don't you dare speak like that in front of the children," Savannah snapped.

"Get rid of the children. What we've got in mind is adults only," said the one wearing a filthy Guns N' Roses T-shirt.

"Matter of fact, we're looking for company tonight," said the one with yellow eyes. Every comment was accompanied by bursts of high-pitched laughter as if each one thought his friends were the greatest comedians ever, and not a bunch of stinking losers. Savannah bit her lip, desperate to say something that would make them wish they'd never been born. But her priority was the children. They were clinging to her hands or the back of her skirt, and she looked around wildly for Garrett.

"Can't wait to try out that juicy ass of yours, mama—"

Savannah relinquished her hold on Opal's hand and slapped the wolf right across his grimy face.

He blinked, staggered back theatrically, then a slow grin spread across his face. "Ohhh… Like it rough do you? So do I. When I've finished with you, you won't know what hit you."

"What's going on here?" Garrett roared, appearing at a run. He squared up the three of them, fists bunched.

"You got a feisty one," said the one she'd slapped, still rubbing his cheek.

Garrett stared at her, appalled. "What did they say to you?"

"Things that are not fit for the children's ears, let alone mine," she said.

"Savannah is the children's nanny. You leave her the hell alone," he warned the three wolves.

"You shouldn't be bringing women into town if you're not going to share," said the one in the Guns N' Roses T-shirt. "This is a shifter community."

Garrett jabbed a finger at him. "You're the last ones to talk about community," he growled.

"What do you mean?" said the one with the yellow eyes. He was the smallest, but meanest of the three.

"Those two," Garrett nodded to the other two wolves. "Hate each other's guts. And you're a great leader for not realizing it, Tyrell."

Tyrell drew back his lips and snarled, revealing rows of pointy yellow teeth. "Don't you dare pass comment on my pack. Especially when you're busy screwing a human."

"I warned you not to make crude comments about her!" Garrett roared, yanking at his T-shirt and jeans.

Before Savannah knew what was happening, his clothes were discarded on the ground and a huge brown bear had burst out of him. It was truly massive. Terrifying, really. Then it stood up on his back legs, towering several feet over them. Its long claws flexed, glistening and deadly, and it drew back its lips and snarled, revealing sharp, white teeth.

The three men didn't wait to remove their clothes. There was a sound of ripping fabric, and, to Savannah's dismay, they transformed into lean, gray beasts with snapping jaws. The whole thing happened in a flash, and she only just had time to drag the three children away and hide them around the back of the truck before Garrett and the wolves met in an almighty clash.

Garret's bear was bigger than the three of them put together, but he was obviously outnumbered as they attacked him on all sides. A single swipe from his huge paws was enough to send them flying, but they hit the ground, and kept coming.

Savannah clamped her hand over her mouth in horror. She'd seen wolf fights before; they weren't pretty. She saw what they were doing—sinking their dirty fangs into his hide over and over, trying to weaken him bit by bit. Death by a thousand cuts.

Opal and Poppy huddled against her, screaming at the wolves to leave Garrett alone.

"It'll be okay," Holt muttered. "Garrett is stronger than all of them." Savannah flashed him a look of gratitude, encouraged by his confidence.

The fight went on and on, getting increasingly vicious, blood flying, and the air thick with roars and yelps of pain.

"Do something," she pleaded with the guy in the truck, who was hunched in the flatbed, watching tensely.

"Can't," he muttered through gritted teeth, fists clenched. "If my animal gets out it'll kill you all." He turned to look at her, his eyes glowing red, and she glimpsed his beast. It was like a black hole of desperation and darkness, and every hair on her body seemed to stand on end. She trembled and held the children tighter. She hated feeling so helpless. Every wound Garrett sustained felt like a stab in her own heart, and all she could do was watch in terror and hope for the best.

CHAPTER 8

Garrett was stronger than the wolves, but collectively they were wearing him down. They were getting smarter, attacking him from behind, staying out of reach of his deadly claws. And he hated that his kids were watching, and so was Savannah.

Screw this. It had to stop right now. With a wild roar, he turned his attack up a gear, slashing Tyrell right across the muzzle. The big wolf yelped and retreated, his face gushing blood. When one of the others turned his head to see what had happened, Garrett slashed his snout open, too.

The third wolf took one look at the carnage and released its hold on Garrett's rear leg. It lowered its head and backed away, and finally, it was over. Tails between their legs, the three of them turned and ran, leaving a trail of blood behind them.

Garrett stood still, panting and checking his injuries. The wolves' teeth were sharp, but his hide was thick, and none of the wounds had cut deep. He didn't want to shift back and let the kids see his injuries, and he really didn't want Savannah to see him naked, but what option did he have?

Keeping his back to them, he enfolded his bear inside him and regained his human form. He snatched up his clothes and pulled them on again, wincing as they caught on his drying blood. Finally, he went over to the children, arms out. He knelt down and they rushed at him, Poppy and Opal sobbing. He wrapped them in his embrace, purring, reassuring them, and they pressed their foreheads against his chest, until their fear had eased away.

He gazed at Savannah over their heads, and the look in her eyes almost stopped his heart. She looked horrified. But more than that…revolted? She'd been disgusted to see him fighting as an animal. He guessed he didn't blame her, but it still hurt.

"Garrett, let's get you home and look at those injuries," she murmured.

"I'm fine," he told her. "Beasts heal fast."

Her eyes flashed. "You're not a beast, Garrett," she said. "You just stood up for me and protected me, that's not what beasts do."

His stomach tingled. *No.* She wasn't revolted. She'd been scared for him. And that touched him deep inside. She looked very sexy like that, all fierce and supportive. But it was only because she didn't really know him. Didn't understand what his beast was capable of.

And what was the point in telling her?

"Let's get back to the house," he said instead.

The kids were quiet and fearful on the way back home, but he assured them that he could've taken out half a dozen wolves if necessary. Nothing was going to take him away from them. Slowly they started to believe him, and all three of them turned soft and sleepy.

"It's the shock," he mouthed to Savannah. "They'll need to nap for a while."

"I'll take them to the bedroom and read them a story while you get cleaned up?" she offered.

"Thanks." He flashed her a look of gratitude.

In the cramped bathroom, he stripped off his clothes and startled at his reflection in the mirror over the washbasin. Those stinking wolves had got him good. There was hardly a patch of skin that wasn't covered in bite marks. He was more red than tan, and the scent of his dried blood nauseated him. He got into the shower and scrubbed himself all over, until every drop of blood was gone, and those filthy fang-marks were fading out.

He was just finishing off, when there was a knock on the door. He wrapped a towel around his waist and opened it.

Savannah was standing there, her eyes huge with worry. "Oh my God," she whispered, scanning his bare torso. She blinked fast, and he was shocked to see that her eyes were bright with unshed tears. "That was so awful. I was so scared for you."

She'd been holding it together for the kids. He understood that now. "Nothing I couldn't handle," he said gruffly, and reached out to rub her shoulder in what was supposed to be a comforting gesture.

But she took another step forward and closed the bathroom door. They were close together in the small, steamy space, and suddenly his arms were around her, while her fingertips skated across his back, as if she was scared to hurt him. His nostrils filled with her scent, that sweet, honeysuckle fragrance, overlaid with the sharper tang of her fear. Her hair was deliciously soft, and he longed to bury his face in it and stay like that for a long time. Instead, he rubbed her back in big circles, rumbling softly, as he did with the kids, and gradually he felt the tension going out of her body.

"I know you're a really tough guy, Garrett," she whispered. "But they were so nasty. And the way they were ganging up on you—" she broke off with a shudder.

He squeezed her a little tighter. His injuries burned, but he didn't care. She felt incredible in his arms, so soft and curvy and feminine. His bear quit rumbling and started up purring, and that meant trouble. Reluctantly, he released her and took a step back. Her pupils were dilated, and she was breathing fast.

"They've been causing trouble for a while now," he said. "The three of them live in a filthy shack on the outskirts of town, but there seem to be other ones coming and going as well. I've got my eye on them, because I'm worried they're up to something bigger."

He hesitated, not sure if he should be sharing the details of Ragtown with her. But she'd been there in the park, protecting his kids like a mother bear, while Ryker was powerless, paralyzed by his beast. She deserved to know. "The other day, someone stole my timber. They were the only ones I suspected, so I went over to get it back. Sure enough, it was there. But there was also a weird smell. It was only later I realized it might have been meth. And that's bad news."

Savannah shivered. "Yeah, it's the worst. Something like that could destroy this town in months."

"I know," he said grimly, wondering if its evil had impacted on her life in some way. "We're going to have to get rid of them. Threatening you today was the last straw. I've got no time for that."

"It was nothing I couldn't handle," she said. "I just wanted them to quit speaking like that in front of the children."

He looked at her in admiration, taken yet again by her tough spirit. "What brought you here?" he blurted out. Then he clicked his tongue. He had no right to ask her questions like that. Having her so close to him was doing crazy things to his head.

"I used to—" she began.

"I'm sorry, I didn't mean to pry."

She blinked fast. "No, it's okay. I had someone once that I thought was my mate. But I was in an accident, and he left me afterwards."

Her eyes were full of pain, and it got him, right in the heart. He hated that she'd suffered, and he found himself wanting to protect her from any future suffering.

She fell silent, eyes downturned, and he suspected there was more to her story, but he wasn't going to push her. He just waited quietly, taking in her features. He liked the way her eyelids were a little darker than the surrounding skin, and her eyebrows had hints of reddish gold.

"I was pregnant at the time of the accident," she said, so quietly that he strained to hear. "Then I lost the baby." There was so much grief in her voice that it pierced him, and he longed to take her in his arms again. He tried to imagine how it felt for her. All he could come up with was imagining how it'd feel if the kids disappeared from his life. "I'm sorry about everything that happened to you. You're a good person, you don't deserve it."

She made a kind of choked sound in her throat. "I thought meeting a man who already had kids would be a perfect fit," she whispered.

"I'm sorry for how things got screwed up here, too," he said.

At last, she looked up and met his gaze. The whites of her eyes were tinged pink, and her lower lip was quivering. "It wasn't your fault."

"But it was me you were looking for. I still don't understand how—"

Her face was open, vulnerable, and she sucked in a breath, as if the same desire that had taken hold of his body was running through hers. His gaze dropped to her mouth, and he let out a groan. He took a step closer, dipped his head, and suddenly they were kissing.

CHAPTER 9

Savannah was too stunned to respond at first, rendered senseless by the feeling of Garrett's mouth on hers. His lips were soft, firm, tender, all at once. He held her around her waist, pulling her close, while she laid her hands gently on his shoulders, avoiding his injuries, and they lost themselves in each other, kissing deeper and deeper. As their tongues danced into each other's mouths, Garrett's hands began to run all over her body, underneath her shirt, cupping her breasts through the fabric of her bra. A flame of desire ran through her body, flaring under his touch. He was hard; she could feel his erection beneath his towel, pressing against her stomach, and it turned her on even more. When her hand wandered down, all of its own accord, and felt the tip of it, he growled into her mouth. She wanted him so bad. Deep inside her. Possessing her. His big hands cupped her ass and he lifted her onto the edge of the sink. He pushed himself between her thighs and she instinctively wrapped her legs around his hips, bringing his erection right against her aching core. His tongue plunged deeper into her mouth and she reached for the top of the towel. She'd gotten it half untucked, when a plaintive voice came from the other side of the door.

"I'm hungry."

They jerked apart, guiltily. Garrett held her for a moment longer, his forehead pressing against hers, and they exchanged wry smiles. Then he tightened the towel around his waist and opened the door.

"I'm bored, too. Opal and Poppy are still sleeping." Holt's eyes were big, and he regarded the two of them curiously.

"Savannah is just dealing with my injuries, Squirt. I'll get dressed, then come cook dinner."

"And then we can play a game together?" Savannah suggested, and Holt's eyes lit up.

He started making airplane noises, and zoomed off down the hallway, holding his arms out to the sides.

When Garrett turned back to her, he couldn't look her in the eye.

"I'd better leave you to it," she said, and rushed out of the bathroom.

Savannah closed herself in her bedroom, and leaned against the door, heart pounding. What just happened? Her body was charged with desire, her skin tingling all over, and she suspected her panties were more than a little damp. She thought he didn't like her that way. He'd told her enough times that he wasn't interested. But he'd kissed her like he wanted to suck the soul out of her body. Like he couldn't get enough of her. And kissing him had felt like the most natural thing in the world.

That whole episode had come out of leftfield. She'd never shared the story of her past with anyone, least of all someone as emotionally unavailable as Garrett. But he'd been kind, and it had encouraged her to open up. It had been a relief to share all the sufferings that had brought her to Ragtown, to explain that she wasn't just some crazy person who didn't care who she mated. She needed him to know that she'd already had a mate, and lost him.

What would've happened if they hadn't been interrupted? That beautiful body of his, naked apart from the towel, hard and ready for her. Her body had cried out for him, yearning for him to mate her. If he'd slipped her panties aside, she wouldn't have stopped him from taking her, right there on the washbasin.

But that would've been a mistake. Because he didn't want a mate. If he mated her, only to reject her again, it would be more than her heart could take. She wasn't about to be his play thing. His nanny with benefits. So what if he was attracted to her?

There's no way it's going to happen again, she told herself, but the thought hurt.

When Savannah slipped into the kitchen, sheepishly, the kids were sitting around the table, bickering with each other, while Garrett was busy cooking a ton of meat on the grill.

"Hi," she said weakly.

Hi, Savannah!" the kids chirped, but Garrett didn't turn around. Her stomach dropped. He regretted it, then. Somehow this was worse than him only wanting her for her body.

Had she forced herself on him? The way she remembered it, it had been the other way around. But the whole thing was a blur. For once in her life, she'd let herself go and been driven by her instincts. And look how it had turned out.

Damn. Her feelings were all over the place. She badly needed to be alone to process them. But instead, she was forced to be here, in the presence of the man who was responsible for throwing them into a spin, while having to act cheerful in front of the kids.

"Need a hand?" she called to Garrett.

"No, I'm good," he grunted.

Oookay then.

"Look what I've made!" Poppy indicated the picture she was drawing with a bunch of colored crayons. Gratefully, Savannah slid into the seat beside her and started making guesses at what all the squiggles were supposed to represent.

Garrett kept his back to the room until all the meat and vegetables were ready, as if he was trying to go as long as possible without looking at her.

When he finally turned around, his jaw was tense and his face was closed. She tried to catch his eye, but he kept his attention focused on the food. When he dumped the stacked trays on the table, she jumped up to grab plates and silverware.

Unfortunately, the way the chairs were arranged meant they ended up sitting directly opposite each other. Garrett was quiet as he dug into his food, while she kept up a nervous stream of chatter with the kids.

She thought she was doing a good job of hiding her emotions, until Opal demanded, "Are you mad at each other?"

"No," Garrett answered quickly.

Opal's eyes turned liquid.

Savannah clasped her chubby little fist. "Of course, we're not mad at each other, honey. There's no reason to be upset."

"B-but if you're not talking to each other, you must be mad at each other," she stammered, her lower lip wobbling.

"That's true," Poppy agreed, and to Savannah's dismay, her lip started to wobble, too.

"Are you going to leave us?" Opal asked, in a high voice that pierced Savannah's soul.

Garrett leapt out of his seat and hugged Poppy and Opal from behind. "Savannah's not going anywhere," he said firmly, but when his dark eyes met Savannah's at last, they were full of questions.

"I'm not," she said, and her stomach tightened another turn. The last thing she wanted to do to those kids was make them a promise she couldn't keep.

Relief showed on Garrett's face, and Savannah startled. Why did he even want her to stay? She was hardly the only nanny in the world.

"Sometimes adults just need quiet time," Garrett continued.

Holt, who had been sitting stoically the whole time, piped up, "Sometimes adults who like each other don't talk to each other."

Garrett's head turned in Savannah's direction and she met his gaze again. His eyes were glowing with an emotion she couldn't read—regret? Hope?

Poppy and Opal seemed satisfied with the answer though.

"Do you like each other?" Poppy asked.

Garrett cleared his throat loudly. "Yes, we're good friends." Then he clapped his hands together. "It's been a long day with plenty of excitement. Let's get you in the bath, and if you're good and don't mess around, Savannah will read you a bedtime story."

The girls ran off happily. "For some reason they love bath-time," Garret told Savannah, with an ironic expression, and fleetingly, there was that connection between them again.

Holt insisted on staying behind to wash the dishes. "And Holt does more than his fair share of the work around here," Garrett said, laying an arm around his shoulders. Holt pretended to knock it off, but Savannah saw that the compliment meant a lot to him.

Savannah stayed with Holt to dry up, and she was relieved when Garrett left them to it. She chatted to him about his passion for racing cars, but her thoughts kept flickering onto the tension between her and Garrett, and how it was affecting the children. When they'd finished, Garrett was still bathing the girls, and then she took the two of them and Holt to their room and read them stories until three pairs of eyes were closed, thick, dark eyelashes splayed on their cheeks.

When Savannah crept out of the bedroom and shut the door, her heartbeat sped up. As much as she hated the idea, she needed to have a conversation with Garrett about what had happened. Clear the air between them, to make sure they didn't act weird around the kids.

But he wasn't in the kitchen. He wasn't in the living room or the bathroom, either. She crept up to his dark bedroom door and listened, guiltily. There was no sound within, but he had to be there. Should she knock? What if he was asleep already? A glance at her watch told her it was only nine p.m.

Hesitantly, she lifted a hand and rapped on the door.

Nothing.

She tried two times more, with the same result.

Was he ignoring her? That was weird, and inappropriate,

considering. With a rush of annoyance, she tried the handle. The door opened. Holding her breath, she peered into the room.

It was empty.

He'd gone out without telling her—but why? She gazed around his room, miserably. It was tidy—military-style tidy with the bed made up perfectly. He didn't answer to her, of course. But this wasn't a normal situation. Ragtown wasn't a normal town. And single men didn't usually kiss their nannies, then act like nothing had happened.

Things suddenly felt a whole lot worse.

CHAPTER 10

The next morning, Garrett was already in the kitchen when Savannah got up. A patch of early-morning light streamed in through the window, illuminating his bare forearms. He was wearing a crisp white T-shirt that looked great against his tan skin. She tried not to notice the way that it outlined his pecs, and how the sleeves were a little tight around his massive biceps.

"Hi," he said, with a casual smile. "How did you sleep?"

She blinked. He was acting like nothing had happened, while her insides were in turmoil. "Not too well," she admitted. That was an understatement. She'd tossed and turned all night, wondering where he was; wondering what she was going to do. The thought of continuing to live with him was unbearable.

"I'm sorry," he said. "I didn't sleep well either." He did look tired, she noticed, with purplish shadows beneath his eyes.

She hesitated, not sure whether to bring up yesterday, now that she'd caught him alone.

"I knocked on your door last night," she said at last. "You weren't there."

Immediately, his face shut down. "I had to go out," he said shortly. "Deal with something in town."

She opened her mouth to ask him to let her know next time he did something like that. But then she closed it again. Did she have a right to make such demands? She didn't know. She had no idea where she stood. Apart from everything else, she'd never even worked as a nanny before.

"We need to be on the same page, for the sake of the kids," she said instead.

He nodded. "Agreed. The conversation at dinner made me realize that we can't go confusing them."

Her heart lurched. "Do you want me to leave?" she said. And to her shame, her voice quavered.

His eyebrows drew together, and he fixed her with a look so serious that the hairs on her forearms stood on end. "I want you to stay. But yesterday was a mistake."

She gulped. "Yes, it was," she said quickly, but the ache in her heart said the opposite. "I think the fight confused things. But we're just friends."

He nodded, looking relieved. "Just friends," he echoed. He went to the cupboard and took out some boxes of cereal.

"Today is my day with the kids," he said, setting them on the table. "They take Fridays off school and I spend the day with them, teaching them practical things and playing games."

"That's nice," she said, forcing a neutral tone.

He turned his head. "Want to join us?"

Her poor heart jolted. All these swift changes of mood were too much for it. "I have to work in the café," she told him. "But I was planning on taking them to an afternoon reading group in the library, if that's okay with you?"

"That's fine," he said, with his head stuck in the fridge. "I'll drop them off later."

* * *

ONCE SAVANNAH HAD HELPED Poppy and Opal to brush their teeth and get dressed in matching tracksuits, she left for the café. To her surprise, there were three customers in there already—Timon and two other men she hadn't seen before. They were sitting at separate tables and not interacting, but at least they were there. Florence was busy reorganizing the library, so Savannah worked by herself in the café.

So, they were just friends. It hurt. It had been a slip. She knew that him wanting her, and him wanting her to be his mate were two different things, and she had to respect that. Still, her thoughts kept escaping to their clinch. How delicious his mouth had felt on hers; how his hands had run all over her body hungrily, but with respect. So different from sex with her ex. Joel had always been seen kissing as no more than a prelude to sex, while Garrett, so big and rough in many ways, had caressed her with such tenderness.

In the afternoon, she happened to be thinking about Garrett, daydreaming about those deep brown eyes, and that rare smile, which when it came was all the sweeter, when the door burst open and he came in, accompanied by Holt, Poppy and Opal. Her heart pounded, but she forced herself to stay calm as she slipped out from behind the counter to hug the kids. When they scampered up the spiral staircase to the library, Garrett said hello, but he didn't hang around to chat, and she was both relieved and disappointed when he left.

Florence scurried downstairs to grab a jug of water and some glasses. "Ready to start?" she asked Savannah excitedly.

"You bet," Savannah replied with more enthusiasm than she felt. "Are Garrett's kids the only children in town?"

"Yup. Unfortunately," Florence replied. "But at least there are three of them, so they don't get lonely."

"I'm sure they'll grow up to be strong and independent," Savannah said.

"Well, they've got a lot of tough role models around," Florence agreed with a chuckle.

The three children sat in front of Savannah, arms and legs folded, as Florence had directed them to, and looked up at her with rapt attention. The book was an adventure story, chosen by Holt.

Savannah opened to the first page, and was about to begin, when Timon appeared at the top of the stairs. She threw him a curious look, and he shrugged.

"I like coming to reading group," he mumbled. He was a strange bear; very quiet, and he kept to himself, but Savannah liked having him around. He sat on a beanbag at the back of the group—as far away from everyone else as he could get.

She cleared her throat and began.

As she read, she was aware of Timon's eyes burning into her. It was a little unsettling being the subject of his laser-beam focus, but she didn't get the hostile vibes from him that she felt from most of the shifters in Ragtown, and she was glad for that. The story involved a large cast of characters, and she enjoyed doing all the different voices for them. The children laughed and shrieked in all the right places, and Timon even let out a little chuckle from time to time.

When she read "the end," and closed the book with a snap, Timon gave a round of applause, and the children joined in.

"Great job!" Florence said with her typical enthusiasm. "Everyone, say thank you to Savannah."

"Thank you," the kids chorused, and Savannah warmed. She'd happily read to them all day long.

"Now, who wants to run around for a little while?" Florence said, no doubt appreciating that the kids would be bursting with energy after such a long period of sitting still. Sure enough, they bounded to their feet and were soon hurtling around the library.

Timon stood up, too. "Uh, I was wondering if I could speak to you," he mumbled.

Savannah looked up from the pile of books that she was rearranging.

"How can I help?" she asked.

"W-well...I-I..." He stuttered. He huffed and puffed, trying to get his question out. Poor guy. He really wasn't a bear of words.

"No rush, Timon, just take your time." She smiled encouragingly.

"I was thinking about opening a pizza place," he managed to get out, after a lot of false starts.

"That's great," she exclaimed.

"Yeah—" he broke off. He lifted up his T-shirt and scratched his belly, before apparently remembering that wasn't an appropriate thing to do in public. He yanked it down again and coughed. "The space next door to the café is vacant, and I was wondering if I could take it over."

"I think that's a great idea. This town could definitely do with a good pizza place," she said slowly, wondering what her part in this was.

"You seem like a smart person, that's why I decided to ask you," he explained. "Florence is a smart person, too, but she gives too much coffee away." He gave a dry laugh. "I've been reading cooking books and trying out different pizzas at home. But it'd be better with a real pizza oven. Holt told me you make great pizza. I was wondering… Maybe you could taste mine and give me your opinion on it?"

"I'd love to," she said genuinely. "Wait, let me ask Florence what she thinks about the business." She scuttled over to Florence and relayed the idea to her.

"I think that's a fantastic idea. Very enterprising. That's if the opinion of such a coffee waster can be trusted," she said, chuckling. She didn't seem at all offended by Timon's comment about her. If anything, she seemed rather proud of it, Savannah noted. She was definitely a quirky person.

"Do you know what the situation is with the place next door? Does Timon need to get a license or anything?"

Florence burst into her chipmunk chuckle again. "No, my dear, that's not how things work here. You see an empty property, you jump on it. It's yours."

Timon gave a rumbling laugh. "I figured that's how it was," he said.

Savannah clasped her hands together. "Okay, great, looks like you'll be opening soon," she told him. His eyes lit up and her mood lifted, for the first time that day. Garrett was confusing the hell out of her, but at least she was doing some good in the town.

CHAPTER 11

Garrett had not been a good parent today. He'd been distracted and short-tempered, and it had taken everything he had to hide it from the kids. None of it was their fault, of course. It was all him—kissing Savannah in the bathroom, when he was wearing nothing but a towel. If Holt hadn't knocked on the door, he wouldn't have been able to control himself. He would've mated her, right then and there, on the bathroom sink.

Savannah. Just the thought of being with her made him hard. The way she'd felt in his arms—all soft and curvy and luscious. But he shouldn't have taken that step. It wasn't fair on her. He'd already told her he didn't want a mate. And now he was confusing her.

Hell, he was confused. His bear insisted she was his. But that could never happen.

He hated the fact that he'd been avoiding her all day. She didn't deserve that either. He'd given her a home then made her feel uncomfortable in it. What kind of asshole did a thing like that?

During dinner, she was cheerful with the kids as usual, and a stranger would only be able to tell something was wrong from the way that she avoided eye contact with him and didn't ask him about his day. They put the kids to bed together, reading a story each, then she went into the kitchen and shut the door behind her.

Garrett paced up and down the corridor. He wondered if she was calling someone, saying that she wanted out of Ragtown. Guiltily, he put his ear to the door, but there was only silence within. He went to his room and tried lying down on his bed, but he couldn't stand it any longer. He stormed back to the kitchen and yanked the door open.

Savannah was sitting at the table, reading some text on her phone. Her hair swung forward like a curtain on her left side, but she'd tucked the other side behind her ear, and she was toying with a loose tendril. She looked up and several emotions crossed her pretty features, too fast for him to pick out a single one. But her overall demeanor was sad. *Shit.* He'd done that to her. She'd told him she'd been rejected, and he'd made her feel worse.

He cleared his throat. "Uh, can we talk?"

Her lips stretched into a smile that didn't begin to reach her eyes. "About what?"

He exhaled slowly. "About my behavior."

She blinked several times, then seemed to compose herself. "Let's pretend yesterday didn't happen. I'm your employee. I care about the kids and giving them a stable life. And that's all."

Garrett frowned. "You really mean that?"

"Uh-huh." She still had that smile fixed to her face. It was nothing like her real, Savannah smile, which was joyous and lovely and lit him up inside.

"Okay then," he said. He turned and left the room.

Five paces along the corridor, he stopped dead.

Then he rushed back to the kitchen. "I can't pretend yesterday didn't happen."

Her features tensed with worry. "Why?"

"It's too big. We've got to talk about it." He knew his tone was brusque, but it was the only way he could deal with emotions like that.

Her lips formed a small O. "Sure. But let's talk outside. I need some air." She got up, but the way she was holding herself looked vulnerable and his chest ached.

He followed her out of the house and around to the rear terrace.

For a while they sat in silence, side by side, watching the last of the day's light reflecting off the gurgling stream.

"Last night was…real. Please don't think it wasn't. But—"

"But you don't want a mate," she said in a singsong voice, and rolled her eyes. "Yup, I think I know that refrain by now."

"I can't be sorry it happened though."

Her head snapped toward him. "You can't?"

"No, not when it felt like that." He fell silent. There was a sound of voices at the front of the house. He stood up and sniffed hard at the evening air. But the breeze was blowing in the wrong direction and he couldn't identify them. "Stay here," he told Savannah. Then, he went around the side of the house, his hackles rising. If it was those wolves again, there was going to be trouble.

Two tall figures were standing with their backs to him. He let out a breath of relief. It was only Jagger and Brock. "Hey, we're out the back," he said quietly, since the kids were asleep.

They turned and followed him.

Jagger greeted Savannah warmly, looking genuinely pleased to see her, while Brock introduced himself.

"Can we speak to you for a minute?" Jagger asked Garret. His heavy jaw was tense, and eyes full of worry.

Garrett glanced at Savannah. He was grateful she'd agreed to speak to him, and now wasn't the time to put off their conversation.

"I'll leave you to it." She was already getting to her feet.

Garrett looked from her, to Jagger and back again, conflict raging inside him. He *was* worried about what the guys had to say to him. The scent of their tension was thick in his nostrils. But it would have to wait. "No—" he began.

"It's okay—we can catch up later. We share a house after all." She chuckled.

He turned to the guys, making a decision fast. "Whatever you have to say to me, you can say in front of Savannah," he told them.

Jagger planted his hands on his hips, relief flashing in his eyes. "Our hunch about the werewolves was right. They are drug dealers. They've approached a few people in the town, trying to sell."

"And that's not all," Brock cut in. "I found a piece of what looks like an explosive device when I was clearing the mine. The collapse was no accident."

"You think they're after the mine?"

Brock nodded. "It's the perfect place for a meth lab."

Garrett frowned. "You're right. There's a lot of space down there. Plenty of privacy. No one's going to notice the smell." He turned to Jagger. "What are you going to do?"

"We've got to get them out of here." He snorted. "We might be a community of broken shifters, but we're not that kind of broken. I just need time to figure out how to do it right."

He clapped his hands together. "Okay, I won't take up any more of you folks' time. But be careful if you're out at the weekend festival."

Garrett nodded. He squeezed Brock's shoulder, then he and Jagger embraced in their usual bear hug, reinforcing the closeness between their animals. With a polite good night to Savannah, the two guys left.

"That's bad news isn't it?" Savannah said as soon as they were gone.

"It is. Those damn meth labs bring in so much money. We're not going to get the wolves out without a fight. I don't even know how many of them there are now."

He glanced at her surreptitiously while she gazed at the water. She didn't look scared, and he was glad for that. But he was worried about the safety of her and the kids. He got to his feet and paced up and down the terrace, grinding his teeth in anger. Just when it seemed like Ragtown was getting half civilized, those walking slimebuckets had to turn up and ruin it for everybody. That was what happened when you tried to create something good—everybody wanted a piece of it.

"You should reconsider staying in Ragtown," he blurted out.

"No," Savannah said quietly, but firmly.

He stopped in front of her. "Savannah, it's dangerous here. You saw that when those wolves attacked me. It's no place for humans. You could end up in a bad situation, and you wouldn't be able to defend yourself. This is a junkyard of feral shifters on their last chance in life. It's not right for you. You're so good and decent. You deserve something better than this. Much better."

To his surprise, she stood up, too, coming within inches of him. "Don't make the mistake of underestimating me, Garrett." She jabbed a finger at his chest, and even in the almost dark, he could see that her eyes were blazing. "I can handle shifters. I've had to deal with my fair share of beasts, you know. And I've survived, largely unscathed." She gave a bitter laugh. "This place is better than where I came from, by a long shot. I'm not going anywhere."

She sat down again and crossed her legs. "Now, what did you want to talk to me about?"

Garrett gazed at her, taken aback by her feistiness. If she was a shifter, she'd be something hella fierce, like a panther, maybe.

Instead, she was the toughest human he'd ever met, bar none.

But that didn't mean she should stay here. What he'd said was true: without her own animal, she was vulnerable to being attacked by any shifter in the town. He thought it was crazy that Florence had decided to live here, but at least she could shift into her squirrel and retreat up to a high place if things got hairy.

"You were telling me how much you liked kissing me," she prompted.

He sighed. What was the point of talking about the kiss now? What he should do was tell her to pack her bags and leave first thing tomorrow.

"I did." He groaned. "But it can't happen again. Relationships are not for me. I'm going to be single for the rest of my life."

"That's a pity, because I think you've got a lot to offer, Garrett," she murmured. There was a seductiveness in her voice that shuddered all the way through him.

"You're wrong. I've got nothing to offer a mate," he said firmly.

"You've never had a mate?"

"Nope."

"What about the kids' mother?"

He started up pacing again. Thinking about the reason why he had become the kids' guardian was always more than he could take. But she deserved to know. He'd been wanting to tell her ever since she'd become their nanny, but he kept putting it off.

"She wasn't my mate. Their father was a close friend of mine, though. He was a great guy. Not like me."

"What do you mean?"

He stayed quiet, the only sound the stomping of his feet on the wooden boards. He wanted to tell her about himself. He didn't know why. It was the first time he'd wanted to talk about what had happened. But it was too much. Too much to share, and too much of a burden to place on her.

"You don't know me. That's why we can't be together. If you did, you'd want nothing to do with me."

"I don't believe that, Garrett." She stood up, blocking his path, and laid a hand on his chest. Close to his heart.

"What are you doing?" he murmured.

"I'm trying to feel your heart. I know it's a good one. You've done such a good thing to take care of the kids."

"I had to. You don't understand." He took hold of her hand, but didn't pull it away.

"So, help me to understand."

His bear purred. The touch of her hand was driving it crazy, and he was touched by her kindness, her reluctance to believe that he could be bad.

Before he knew it, he was kissing her again, his hands sliding around her narrow back, pressing her against his body.

Her mouth was small and soft, and the touch of her tongue lit a burning trail all the way to his loins. His bear swelled beneath his skin, urging him to mate her, while his hands ran all over her, taking in the lush curves of her hips, the softness of her belly, then going beneath her shirt, skating over the swell of her breasts. She was so petite and feminine, yet her kisses were fierce, and the scent of her desire rose to his nostrils. When his thumbs chafed her nipples, she moaned, and the self-control that he'd been clinging to dissolved.

Hardly aware of what he was doing, he lifted her clean off her feet. She looped her arms around his neck, as if they'd kissed like that a hundred times before. He loved feeling her whole weight in his arms, her soft hand stroking the stubble of his jaw. *Mine*, his bear told him. He was going to mate her, to make her his.

He drew back. "Inside," he growled.

He began to walk her around the house, but she wriggled to get free. "Garrett?"

"What is it?" He looked down at her big eyes and parted lips.

Her expression had turned serious. "You know what you're doing, right?"

Disappointment crashed through him as he stopped walking and put her down gently. "I do," he replied. "And you need to know who I really am, before you decide if you want anything more."

A gust of breeze blew past and she shivered and hugged herself. "Let's go inside."

As they walked into the house, he resisted the urge to put his arms around her, or whip his shirt off and give it to her. It would just make things harder than they were already.

He was shocked when she went straight to his bedroom, but he didn't stop her from going in and perching on the edge of his bed. She leaned back, propping her weight on her elbows. Christ. She looked so enticing like that. He had an overwhelming urge to kneel in front of her, strip her panties off and lick her.

But after he told her his story, she would probably be disgusted at the idea of him touching her. The thought of her being sickened by him knotted up his gut, but he pressed on, knowing he had to. He sat beside her, but as far away as possible, and began:

"I told you my bear was bad—"

She shook her head, disbelieving. But he held up a finger to stop her.

"I'm the son of a violent bear, who was more animal than human. He was a stray, never had a clan of his own because none would take him. But he had a taste for blood. And all he cared about was fighting and killing. It was as if every kill gave him strength. He always stunk of it—blood and death." He swallowed as the memory of that awful stench rose up again.

"He got into fits of rage at the smallest provocation. When my older brother, Jed, and I got to about eight or nine, he started taking it out on us as well. Before we'd even started to shift, he used to beat us black and blue. It got worse and worse through our teens, until one day, he had a drunken blackout and ended up killing Jed—"

Savannah gasped. Her eyes had been getting bigger and bigger, but to his surprise, she shuffled across the bed and laid a hand on his. "His own son? My God, that's awful. It must have destroyed you."

"It did." He dropped his gaze to his lap, the familiar shame coursing through him again. "I was there when it happened, but I wasn't strong enough to fight him off. He half-killed me as well. But here I am today, while Jed, the best brother a bear could ask for, is dead."

Savannah squeezed his hand tighter. "You can't blame yourself for that," she said softly. He blinked, startled that she'd tuned into his feelings so easily.

He let out a sigh. "A million times, I've thought, what if? What if I'd had a weapon? He was always starting fights with us, out of nowhere. We should have had a better plan to protect ourselves. What if I'd run out of the house and gone to get help instead?" He laughed mirthlessly. "Hell, called the human police force. But we'd been raised to believe that family sorts its own problems out. At that point I didn't even know that other bears lived in clans. It was just me, Jed, and our insane father."

"What happened after you lost your brother?" Savannah asked in a whisper.

"My father locked me in the basement until my injuries healed. If I was a human, I probably wouldn't have made it, but my shifter blood got me through in the end. I had a month or more to think about my brother, and I vowed to avenge his death. When my father came to feed me, I made out that I was weaker than I was, still crippled. And when I finally got my strength back, I waited for him to come and feed me one day, and… and I took him out."

He broke off and looked at Savannah, checking that she understood what he was saying. Waiting for her to freak out and run away.

But all she said was, "You did what you had to do. You should be proud of yourself for that, and you've honored your brother's memory."

His heart flooded with gratitude. She was a human, but she understood shifters. Their codes of honor, and the sometimes brutal decisions they had to take.

"Then what did you do?"

"I went feral for a while, living in a forest, fighting anything that challenged me. Until one day, I got sick of living like an animal, and I enlisted in a black ops division of the military that specializes in assassinations of sensitive targets. Jed had encouraged me to be ambitious, and I believed killing was the only thing I was good for. I wanted to put all the rage that was inside me to good use. I was very successful for a long time, removing enemy forces from circulation with zero civilian casualties. The military used me as their ultimate killing machine. Then one day, an operation went badly wrong—"

He broke off and swallowed hard as his throat convulsed with emotion. "My best friend, Slade, had recently lost his mate in a mall shooting. He was in a bad way, and he turned to self-medication. He was high all the time, and I should've reported him, but I didn't want to betray him. Anyway, we were preparing to take out the leader of a guerrilla army in his own house. I was ten feet behind Slade, and had the target in my sights. I pulled the trigger, just as Slade left his position to try to get a better shot. I shot him dead. Blew his brains out. He was my only true friend. And I killed him. I kill anyone I care about."

Savannah sighed. "I don't think that's true, Garrett. It was just very bad luck," she murmured.

He was amazed to discover that she was still touching him. She hadn't yet recoiled.

"I went mad with guilt," he forced himself to continue, even though each word was like a brick, crushing his soul. "The black-ops division kicked me out, because I got unreliable, and I went on a rampage of self-destruction, until I moved to Ragtown after a bear I met in a down-and-out bar told me about it.

"Soon after, the authorities contacted me about Slade's three orphaned children, asking if I'd be willing to become their legal guardian."

Savannah gasped. "You're looking after Slade's children? That was a beautiful thing to do."

He shook his head savagely. "It was my duty. There was no way I would have refused. I carry the burden of their grief on my shoulders every day."

Savannah shuffled even closer, and laid her hand on his upper thigh. "Garrett, listen to me. As you've explained it, Slade's death was not on you. If you want to blame anyone, blame whoever killed his mate. He moved out of position because he was high, right?"

Garrett nodded. "But I knew he was high. I shouldn't have let him go in front of me. It would have been better if he was behind me, and he shot me instead."

"No!" Savannah threw her arms around his neck. "It would not have been better. None of this is your fault. You've got to stop carrying this guilt around."

He allowed himself a second to inhale the sweet, warm scent of her neck. It smelled like comfort and safety. He drew back. "Guilt, bad blood. It's all the same. I'm screwed up. That's why I came up to Ragtown, to live my life out of harm's way. I didn't bank on having the kids of course, but I love them as if they were my own. And then some mysterious matchmaker threw a small curvy human in my path as well."

Savannah stroked his face again. It felt nice. More than nice.

"I don't deserve you." His voice hardened. "I'll only ruin you."

Her forehead furrowed, making her look adorably fierce. "Maybe I should be the judge of that. Maybe a girl who's lost everything is exactly what you need."

"Why don't you go back to that matchmaker of yours and ask her to choose a less screwed up bear for you?"

She rolled her eyes dramatically. "I did, after you were so goddamn friendly that first night. But that crazy lady kept insisting you were the one."

"How could she even know that?" he murmured, running his eyes over Savannah's lovely face. If he had to describe his perfect woman, Savannah would be that, and more. Those pretty eyes, so full of strength and goodness; those sweet round cheeks, and those pretty lips, always ready to curve into a smile or mischievous grin. And that body, which was now pressing against his, working his bear into an uncontrollable need. Controlling it right now felt like holding back a raging tide.

"I want to be with you, but I'm scared what my beast of a bear could do to you," he said through his teeth.

"I'm not scared." She tipped her head back with a defiance that connected directly with his loins. "I've known dangerous men before and they feel nothing like you. You might be broken, and that's understandable. But I think we can do some good for each other." She leaned in and kissed him on his cheek, just where his stubble began. Then she kissed his other cheek, and his nose. She kept going, peppering his face with light, teasing kisses, as delicate as butterflies' wings.

Finally, he angled his head so the next one met his lips. She gave a soft moan that vibrated through him. Then, bracing herself on his shoulders, she climbed astride his lap.

He growled low in his throat as her soft, warm core brushed against his crotch. Instantly, he was hard. Her loose, floaty skirt was all rucked up, and the only thing between them was her panties and his jeans. Taking his head in her hands, she began to kiss him deeply, her sensual pink tongue probing his mouth while her pelvis began to rock, back and forth, across the bulge in his pants. *Holy crap.* Did she know what she was doing? He was going to come in his pants if he didn't manage to rein himself in. His bear was bristling beneath the surface, its hide making his skin burn. He cupped her ass with his hands. It was round and peachy, and barely covered by a scrap of lacy fabric. He loved the way her hair fell over his face, curly and unrestrained, and he loved even more the way she pulled up her shirt and drew it right over her head, before pressing her full cleavage to his face.

Deftly, he unfastened the catch in the back of her bra then slid it from her shoulders, liberating her breasts. Her nipples were dusky pink and already hard as pebbles. When he took one into his mouth, she moaned and clung to him tighter.

Suddenly, she reached for his hand, and pressed it between her thighs. *Christ.* She was already soaking wet. Wet for him. At the thought, his bear unleashed a growl. "Sorry." He drew back, worried she'd freak out.

"I love it. It's sexy," she murmured. She pressed harder on his hand, and he pushed her drenched panties aside and slid two fingers inside her. She gasped into his mouth and his cock surged. He felt her clenching around him, so slick and slippery and ready for him.

He moved his fingers in and out of her, teasingly, and she reached for his T-shirt and tugged it over his head. "You feel incredible," he muttered.

"You do." Her hands were everywhere, caressing his bare torso, lightly scratching his back, driving his bear wild.

At last, she reached for his zipper, unfastened it, and his cock sprung out, rock hard. He slid his fingers out of her and she lifted up, scooted closer, and suddenly she was descending onto him. He watched her face as he entered her, her pupils dilated with pleasure, lips parted, her muscles gradually yielding to his girth. She was already close; he felt the little, tell-tale spasms. He held her ass, pulled her down, until he hit home with a groan of pleasure. They kissed passionately, and he held her tight as he thrust into her, long and deep. She sighed and gasped and shuddered, and he learned what she needed from the jolts of her hips.

Soon, her breathing got faster and faster, and she exploded, trembling all over and moaning into his ear.

He held her tight, moving nice and easy until she was done and falling, limp as a rag doll, onto his shoulder. He lifted her up and laid her down gently on the bed. "A bear takes its mate naked," he growled. He discarded his jeans then slipped off her skirt and panties, exposing her bare body to his gaze. She was beautiful, all curves, and that neat little triangle between her thighs only a little darker than the hair on her head. He bent his head and licked her as he'd been dying to ever since she walked into his bedroom. She tasted honey-sweet, with a hint of salt, and when his tongue met the little pink bud of her clit, she cried out, then laughed at the strength of her own reaction.

"I think it's too soon," she whispered. But he was determined to have her come in his mouth, and he gave her feather-light licks until he sensed she was ready, her arousal beginning to build again. As she got closer and closer, she gripped his head hard, keeping him just where she wanted him. It was damn sexy. He loved her confidence. She shook all over as she came, stifling her cries with a hand over her mouth.

"Come here, make me yours," she whispered.

Garrett didn't need any more encouragement. He arched over her, spreading her thighs wide, and a moment later he was deep inside her again. She was perfect; so soft and eager. Her arms and legs wrapped around his body, holding him tight. He thrust deep, going harder and faster as his bear took over, and she moaned and cried in pleasure. His mouth skated over the side of her neck, every nerve in his body urging him to give her the mating mark that would bind them forever. But he couldn't do it. All he could do was give her the pleasure she deserved.

At last, he couldn't hold back any longer, and with a roar, he came deep inside her, his life force spilling from him to her.

It was the most intense orgasm of his life—because it had

touched his soul as well as his body. When he finally lifted his head, he sensed Savannah felt the same, her eyes glistening with unshed tears.

"Are you okay?" he murmured.

She grinned. "I'm better than okay." He eased himself off her and held her in his arms. She seemed sleepy, giving adorable little yawns and sighs, while Garrett was too stunned to think about moving.

She cared for him. After all those fucked up things he'd just told her, she still wanted to mate him. She didn't think he was a monster. He inhaled the scent of her skin, scarcely able to believe what had just happened. She wasn't naïve; he knew that. She'd listened to him and decided he was still someone she wanted to be with. The thought blew his mind.

Savannah turned onto her back and stretched. "I suppose I should go before I fall asleep," she said, but her voice was full of reluctance.

"No, stay here—" he started to say.

She laid a hand on his forearm. "It's better if I go. I don't want to confuse the kids."

"You're right." He got up and helped her find her clothes. He helped her to put them on again, too, but he'd never dressed a woman before, and it wasn't easy in the dark, and they wound up laughing helplessly.

At the door, he took her in his arms and gave her one final kiss.

"You won't regret this tomorrow?" she whispered.

"Of course not." He raised her hand to his lips and she crept out, back to her own room.

CHAPTER 12

A bear takes its mate naked...

"Penny for your thoughts?"

"What?" Savannah looked at Florence in time to catch the knowing grin spreading across her face. Savannah's cheeks warmed. She shook her head. "Sorry, I was a little distracted. What did you say?"

"Nothing, my dear. I was just wondering what was keeping you so occupied this morning." Florence patted her arm.

Savannah's cheeks got even hotter. "Oh, nothing. I just didn't sleep much last night." Which was true. After she'd returned to her own bedroom, her body had been deeply relaxed, but her brain was wired, constantly replaying every delicious moment she'd shared with Garrett.

"Something keeping you awake?" Florence's head was tilted to the side, her eyes owlish with curiosity.

Savannah laughed nervously. "No, I'm just a bad sleeper sometimes."

"Mmm...hmmm," Florence said. Evidently not fooled for a moment. *Dammit.* How did she know? Could she smell it on her?

Savannah often forgot that Florence was a shifter. Did squirrels even have a strong sense of smell?

Florence turned her attention back to the cake stall that they were setting up for the festival and Savannah gazed at her absently, wishing she could talk to her about last night. In the past—in another lifetime—she'd loved gossiping with her girlfriends about the guys they were dating. And on the whole, she trusted Florence. But she just couldn't shake the feeling that she was hiding something, and that it might be dangerous to say too much about her feelings for Garrett.

Instead, she busied herself with cutting up a coffee cake into slices. The festival was going well. Far better than she'd expected. It was a beautiful day, sunny, but not too hot, with an almost cloudless sky. In addition to the coffee and cake stall, Timon had constructed a small home-made pizza oven out of a bunch of bricks, and the first pizza of the day was currently cooking. It wasn't so much a festival, as a gathering of a handful of people, but Florence was justifiably proud of herself for organizing it. Savannah was proud of her, too, but her thoughts were constantly drifting to Garrett.

A bear takes its mate naked.

The words turned over and over in her brain, sending little tremors of yearning through her body. Did that mean he thought of her as his mate? It sure sounded like it. And yet, he hadn't given her a mating mark. Not that she was aware of anyway. Last night had been so unexpected. But it had felt so right. Garrett was such an amazing lover, and there had been so much passion and tenderness in his eyes. Surely he knew how she felt, and he wouldn't have mated her unless it meant something to him. *Right?* She glanced at Florence wistfully, wishing she could ask her opinion. She seemed to know Garrett better than most.

Every time a guy appeared in Savannah's peripheral vision, she looked up, with her heart beating a little faster, hoping it was him.

She hadn't seen him since last night, having deliberately snuck out of the house before he was up. She'd been scared to see him again. Scared to see a blankness in his expression which would have shattered her heart into pieces. She was so glad he'd opened up to her last night. She understood him a lot better now, understood the pain that had made him deprive himself of a mate for all those years. He'd suffered so much tragedy in his life, but he hadn't done anything wrong. Now, she just hoped that he'd trust her, and come to believe that he deserved a mate, because he was a good man.

But what if he didn't? What if he rejected her yet again? The thought made her stomach turn over.

Well, she'd leave. She couldn't stand to live in Ragtown without him.

"Savannah!"

She turned in the direction of the voice. Timon was waving at her and, for the first time ever, he was smiling. She couldn't help smiling too. She ducked out from behind the cake stall and went over to him. A 16-inch pizza was sitting on a table beside the pizza oven, topped with mozzarella, tomato slices and pepperoni. It had a thin crust, which was perfectly cooked, and it smelled mouth-watering.

"Wow, that looks amazing. Well done, Timon," she said.

Timon dropped his head shyly, but he looked pleased. "Not bad, huh?"

"I've never seen better," she said, and meant it. "You've got real talent."

"Care to try a slice?" he said in his slow voice.

"Would I ever!"

To her surprise, he pulled out a genuine pizza wheel. He must have ordered it specially. Expertly, he cut the pizza into twelve slices, levered a slice onto a sheet of cardboard, and passed it to her.

She blew on it and dug in. It was delicious, and she told him so.

"Thanks, Savannah. Couldn't have done it without you," he mumbled.

"I didn't do anything," she said, laughing. "This is all you."

He shrugged. "You believed in me. That does a lot for a big old bear like me."

She reached out and squeezed his arm. "Well if I've helped, I'm very glad. But you should be proud of yourself....oh, and I think you've got your first customers." She indicated Brock and two other guys who'd appeared beside her.

She returned to the cake stall to help Florence, happy to see that three people were lining up to be served.

Suddenly, her heart clenched so hard she thought it was going to stop altogether.

There was Garrett. On the far side of the park, with Poppy, Opal and Holt. Thankfully, he wasn't looking in her direction. There was a large cardboard box beside him, and he was helping the children arrange what looked like a bunch of paint pots. As she watched, adrenaline racing through her veins, Poppy put out a sign. Savannah squinted. It read, *Face painting – $1*. Opal started painting Poppy's face, while Garrett supervised her, and Holt stood with his hands jammed in his pockets, looking embarrassed. That was cute. The kids had obviously come up with the idea for the stall by themselves, and Garrett was encouraging them. Her heart bloomed with warmth for him. He was such a great dad; she just knew he'd be the perfect mate as well. He was looking as hot as ever in a pale-blue T-shirt and faded jeans. He also looked like he hadn't slept so much last night, with dark shadows beneath his eyes, but it suited him, giving him an air of sexy dishevelment. Yet again, an image of their lovemaking sprung into her mind. Of him deep inside her, his mouth searing hers. *Crap.* And just like that, she was all turned on again.

She shook her head. She had to get ahold of herself and stop staring at him like a pervert. Instead, she focused on serving what was becoming a never-ending stream of customers.

She forced herself to be chatty and friendly, introducing herself to each customer and asking what their name was. Most of them were gruff and standoffish, but she sensed that this would ease once they got to know her better. From time to time, she felt—rather than saw—Garrett's eyes on her. What did that mean? Was he looking at her longingly or regretfully?

She was so deep in thoughts of him that when he finally appeared in front of her, she jumped guiltily.

"Hey," he said with a casual smile that showed his nice, white teeth. Instantly, she lit up inside like a hundred fairy lights.

"Hey, yourself," she managed to say, her heart pitter-pattering beneath her ribcage.

Garrett's deep brown eyes bored into hers, communicating all the things he was unable to say with Florence standing beside her. Relief flooded through her. He didn't regret last night. He was looking at her as if he wanted to take her to bed and do it all over again.

"Looks like we missed each other this morning," he said. His tone was even, but the little tug at the corner of his lips was mischievous.

While Florence was busy dispensing coffees, Garrett ran his eyes all over Savannah's figure, lingering on the inch of exposed cleavage at the top of her floral blouse. It was hot being looked at like that, and a flame of desire ran through her. She wished he could drag her home and tear her clothes off again.

"I had an early start," she murmured. It wasn't easy to hold his gaze, but she forced herself to stare into those burning pools of need. *Damn.* It was insane how much her body wanted him. How much her soul needed him.

"Sleep well?"

"Took me a while to get off, but after that, yes. And you?"

He grinned, evidently enjoying the game they were playing. "Same. I had some pretty unusual dreams though."

Savannah opened her mouth to ask what kind of dreams, but thought better of it. She had a feeling that they involved her, naked. She cleared her throat. "Can I offer you some coffee? Cake?"

"I'll take a coffee. And I'll bring the munchkins over later for some cake. But they've been bugging me to ask if you'll join us for an open-air movie screening later."

"Here?" She gazed dubiously at the scrubby patch of grass where the festival was being held.

"Yeah, Ryker managed to get hold of a generator and we've got a projector and screen."

"What's showing?"

"Ah, that's still up for debate. Probably something involving superheroes and, or mermaids."

"Sounds like my favorite type of movie," she said and they both laughed. "I'll try to make it, but I need to see how work goes."

Okay, we'll hope to see you around four p.m., then," he winked at her, took the cup of coffee and strode back to the kids.

She watched him go, drinking in the sight of his broad shoulders beneath his T-shirt, and the nice shape of his ass. A little part of her had been certain that he'd decide last night was a terrible mistake. But he seemed… happy. Lighter than she'd seen him before.

Did that mean…he wanted them to be together? She couldn't let her thoughts run away with themselves, she knew that. But, oh, she wished so much that this was just the beginning of things. She hoped against hope that he wasn't playing with her heart, encouraging her to spend more time with him and the kids if he wasn't interested in making her his mate.

Was it even a good idea to spend more time in that cozy family group than her role as nanny required?

* * *

Garrett

WITH THE KIDS safely occupied arranging the seats in front of the movie projector screen, Garrett chatted to Callan, Ryker and Brock. Recently, too many of their conversations revolved around the problems in the town. But his attention was only half on them, and kept slipping away to Savannah, who looked so pretty and capable dispensing coffees and slices of cake with her usual good humor. His bear didn't appreciate the way the other shifters were staring at her. And all of them were staring at her. Who could blame them? She was the prettiest, sexiest thing he'd ever seen. And not only that, but she was the only female in town, save Florence. His senses were on high alert. It was dangerous here, and he needed to protect her. Did she realize how much attention she was getting? He doubted it. She smiled and chatted with everyone, but the way she'd looked at him when he'd approached made him feel ten-feet tall. He wished he was normal, like any other bear, and he could let himself fall for her. He'd be giving her a mating mark in no time. Hell, he would have done it already, the first night he'd met her.

Ryker got him caught up in one of his monologues on supply-chain management, so he missed the moment when Savannah approached, and he didn't realize she was there until he picked up that sweet, honeysuckle scent.

"Okay, we're all sold out of cake, so looks like I can watch the movie with you guys," she said brightly.

Garrett couldn't restrain a grin from spreading across his face. "Great. We tossed a coin and *The Twin Mermaids* won." He put an arm around Holt's shoulders. "Sorry, kiddo."

Holt shrugged. "Can't win them all," he said, with a maturity beyond his years.

"We'll watch your pick at home soon," Savannah assured him, and he brightened.

"I'm hungry, let's get pizza," Callan announced, rubbing his stomach. The other guys agreed they'd eaten enough pizza today to fuel a truck, but Savannah said she was hungry, and she and Callan went over to Timon's pizza oven.

Garrett watched as she gave her order and chatted to Timon. The quiet, reclusive bear lit up at the sight of her, and Garrett's hackles rose. Timon wanted her; of course, he did. What if she was better suited to him instead—?

No. He cut that thought off. He wasn't about to see Savannah mated to another shifter in town. *No way.*

Savannah returned with a slice of ham and mushroom pizza, while Callan had an entire pizza to himself. Garrett finished setting up the movie, and the title sequence began to play. The guys let off a collective groan.

"Think I'll pass on the movie and go get beer instead," Callan said. Ryker and Brock agreed.

"Catch you later," Garrett said, secretly relieved. He wasn't having an easy time with his bear, and the fewer guys who were around Savannah, the better. The kids sat down on a blanket, and he and Savannah sat on a couple of beanbags that he'd borrowed from the library. He wasn't a fan of mermaids either, but he'd sat through a hundred cartoon movies over the years, happy to see how much pleasure the kids took from them. Poppy and Opal's eyes were huge with anticipation, their tiny hands folded in their laps as they sat cross-legged. Savannah's beanbag touched the edge of his, but she was a good twelve inches away from him. She was quiet as she ate her pizza. Maybe she was tired from her day's work. Either that, or she was trying to keep her distance from him after last night.

Opal and Poppy shushed everyone and the movie began to play. Immediately, Garrett's attention drifted from the screen to all the guys in the vicinity. Savannah was watching the movie, and the guys were watching her. He would have thought it was surreal if it wasn't so damn aggravating. His bear kept letting out little growls, and he coughed in an effort to hide them.

Just then, Aidan appeared and sat down cross-legged, behind the children and on Savannah's right flank. The hairs on the back of Garrett's neck stood up, and he gave a deliberate, low growl. Aidan's head snapped in his direction, eyes full of innocent surprise. Garrett growled again, and Aidan shuffled at least two feet away, shooting him wounded glances.

This was how it was going to be until he made some kind of public claim on her. But how could he do that?

Garrett made a quick decision. His hand shot out and reached for Savannah's. Her face showed surprise, followed by pleasure, as her soft, small fingers slid into his. He drew himself up and rearranged the beanbags until they made a double seat where they could sit together, and he wrapped an arm around her shoulders.

She snuggled against him and carried on watching the movie as if they'd sat like that a thousand times before. His bear purred, and she made an adorable sound of appreciation.

When her attention was turned away from him, he looked around and glared at every single shifter in the vicinity until their gazes dropped and they skulked away. He didn't care if they started whispering about him. He didn't care what anyone thought. The most important thing was to keep Savannah safe. It felt so good holding her like that; pretending to be a normal guy.

Now, more than ever, he wished he was.

* * *

THE MORNING AFTER THE FESTIVAL, Garrett, Brock, Callan, Aidan, Ryker and Timon met at Jagger's house.

The wolves had to leave town. Jagger had decided.

Garrett was glad for the decision. They'd appeared last night just as the movie was finishing, and had hung around, making everyone uncomfortable. Jagger was doing his best to get Ragtown more civilized, and they were bent on undoing all his hard work. Garrett felt that the children weren't safe around them, and neither was Savannah.

"We'll just go over there, and tell them straight," Jagger said.

Ryker snorted. "Like that's gonna work."

"That's the first step," Garrett said. "And if they don't leave…well there's a lot more of us than of them."

The seven of them flexed their muscles in a show of solidarity and headed over to the wolves' house.

Tyrell and his sidekicks took their time when Jagger banged on their front door. But when Jagger threatened to break it down, and the house with it, they finally appeared, looking meaner and dirtier than ever.

"What the hell you want?" Tyrell demanded, releasing a cloud of stinking breath.

Jagger leaned against the door frame, while the other guys

backed him up. "As Sheriff in this community, I've come to tell you that you aren't welcome here, and I need to ask you all to leave," he said.

Tyrell huffed and spat on the floor. "Last time I checked this was a free country, and we can live wherever we want."

Garrett slammed a fist into his opposite hand with a clap that made all three of the wolves jump. "You could—if you were playing by the rules. But you're a bunch of drug-dealing assholes, and you need to go."

Tyrell smirked. "I'll do a deal with you. We'll go, all right. Just as long as you let us take that hot piece of ass with us."

Pure rage coursed through Garrett's veins, and he bunched his fists to stop his bear from bursting out of him. Somehow, he managed to keep his voice calm. "You're not taking anything from here, besides your criminal asses."

One of Tyrell's sidekicks gave a high-pitched laugh from behind Tyrell's shoulder. "You better be careful how you're speaking to us. You've got children. Or someone's children, anyway."

The bones on Garrett's face began to crack and broaden, and his skin burned as his fur pushed through. "I'll tell you this one time." He jabbed a finger at the three of them. "You mention my kids again, and you're dead. You hurt anyone I care about, you're also dead. I'll put all three of you down without thinking about it."

"And I'll support that," Jagger added. "You got three days to clear out of here. No more warnings."

A heaviness sat deep in Garrett's gut as he stormed back to his own house, forcing his bear down with every ounce of his strength. He didn't know how he'd managed to restrain himself from ripping them apart. Three years earlier, he wouldn't have, and there would've been carnage. He was beyond furious at the insinuations about Savannah and threats toward his children, and he was worried about what the next three days would bring. They obviously weren't going to leave without a fight. But what worried him more was who he became around them.

CHAPTER 13

The kids were at school, the house was tidy, and Savannah was sitting at the kitchen table, with the breeze blowing through the open window. She was reading a brand-new thriller by one of her favorite authors, but she was having a hard time concentrating. Because Garrett was in the house, too. He was working on the doorframe of the guest room, replacing the old, rotten wood, so the door would close properly. Every nerve in her body, every square inch of skin, was aware of him.

From time to time, he drifted in and out of the kitchen, making coffee, grabbing a snack, and his presence had the force of an electric shock. While pretending to be buried in her book, she yearned for him to talk to her, but he was quiet and uncommunicative.

When he came in and stuck his head in the fridge, she asked, "What's wrong?"

He turned and gave her a look she struggled to interpret, but she thought he was pleased she was speaking to him.

"Oh, I'm just worried I'm behind with the renovation work," he said. "The kids need a better home than this collapsing bunch of wood, and I need to get finished before the winter comes. It can get brutal up here, with a lot of snow falling."

Savannah nodded sagely. "Looks like you've made good progress the last few days though?"

He grunted agreeably.

"But what else is bothering you?" she said, a challenge in her voice.

Garrett gave a terse laugh. "How are you so good at reading me?" He shook his head slowly. There was admiration in his eyes, and it warmed her.

"It's because we have a connection," she said simply.

His lips formed a hard line and his expression turned inscrutable again. *Okay.* He didn't want to talk about that.

"We asked the wolves to leave town, this morning," he said.

Disappointment flickered in her at the change of subject. "How did they take it?" she forced herself to say.

He snorted. "About how you'd expect. They pretty much said they weren't going to leave without a fight." He frowned. "Be careful until they've gone. I've got a bad feeling they might try and take revenge on the town. On us."

She nodded. "I'll make sure I don't go out by myself."

"That's good."

She watched him as he took a hunk of cooked meat out of the fridge and cut it into slices. Just like that, he'd closed down again.

"Will you and the guys be able to get rid of them?" she prompted.

"Yeah. Don't worry about that. There's at least eight guys in the town I can count on."

"Will you fight them again?"

"If we have to. But I hope they'll have the sense to know when they're outnumbered."

"You guys are doing a great job dealing with them."

"Thanks," he said shortly.

He wasn't interested in talking. *Fine then.* She picked up her book and leafed to the last page she'd read.

Suddenly, he was beside her, perching on a chair. "Thanks for talking to me." He laid a hand on her arm, his gaze intense.

She looked into those deep brown eyes, and her heartbeat

instantly sped up. "Any time," she murmured. His irises were almost black, but she could just make out the pupils, dilated. And there was a soft purring sound coming from deep inside his broad chest. His lips were parted, inches from hers and she yearned to lean forward and kiss him.

It shouldn't happen again. It was only going to lead to heartbreak. When he'd put his arm around her yesterday during the movie, she felt like she'd lifted right up, floating in space ecstatically. But when the movie ended, he dropped his arm and acted like nothing had happened. That was Garrett: hot and cold. Nothing bothering him too much. Meanwhile, her heart was already wide open to him, and his rejection had the power to cut her to the quick.

"We shouldn't be sitting so close," she whispered.

"You're right," he replied, but his eyes remained locked on hers, with that unwavering intensity.

"I don't want to fall for you, Garrett," she murmured.

"Then I don't want you to either, Savannah." A smile tugged at the corners of his lips. And his mouth was on hers again. Slow, tender, then burning with need.

In another moment, she was on his lap, his arms wrapped around her, his kisses hard and hungry.

Effortlessly, he lifted her up and carried her to his bedroom.

Soon, their clothes were off, and their naked bodies were entwined. His cock was huge and hard against her stomach, and she ached to have him inside her. But this time, she took him in her mouth, teasing him, making him wait. At the first touch of her lips, he groaned and shuddered all over. "What are you doing to me, Savannah?" he murmured, and the words were like a direct connection to her clit. She loved giving him pleasure like that, taking him in deep, imagining what he was going to feel like inside her again.

At last, he gently pulled away from her, turned her onto her front, and entered her from behind. He stroked her ass, whispering compliments as he thrust slowly into her. It was wild and sexy. She'd never liked that position before, but it felt right with him.

He drew her up, holding her against his body and caressing her breasts and clit until the motion of his cock deep inside her tipped her right over the edge. With no one to hear them, she came with a cry that seemed almost animal to her own ears, and his bear purred its approval.

Once her orgasm had died away, Garrett got rougher and faster, as if he was finally letting himself go. And she loved it. Loved taking all he had to give her. She laid her head on her hands as he held her hips and ploughed into her, fierce and strong and animalistic. He let out a bear's roar as he came, ejaculating deep inside her.

He collapsed on the bed and drew her into his arms. "I'm sorry. I lost control. I hope I didn't hurt you?" His eyes were soft now, and full of worry.

"Don't be sorry. You didn't hurt me. I loved it," she reassured him. "I love feeling your animal."

"You turn me on so much. I couldn't hold back." He buried his face in the side of her neck, inhaling her scent. Their skin was slick with perspiration, and she loved the way they slipped against each other, his skin soft against hers. He didn't seem in any hurry to leave, but held her in his arms, worshipping her body with his words and caresses.

"If I didn't know any better, I'd think you were falling for me, Garrett," she said playfully.

He stilled and raised an eyebrow. "I could say the same thing about you, Savannah," he said.

A shiver went all the way through her. Could it be true? She hoped so, more than anything.

* * *

Garrett

THERE WERE plenty of things he should be doing right now, but none of that mattered. Savannah was lying in his arms again, naked and delicious. She was perfect for him in every way. And his bear was convinced that she was his mate. But his animal couldn't be trusted. It was clawing at him, urging him to give her a mate mark, when all he wanted was to lie there and enjoy the moment for as long as possible.

His skin was burning like crazy and he sat up abruptly. "I need to go for a run in the woods," he told her.

Disappointment passed across her lovely features, but she pulled herself together fast. That's how she was: resilient and good-natured. And he was glad he didn't have to explain the effect that she was having on his bear.

"Can I come?" she asked.

He blinked. "Why?" he blurted out before he could stop himself.

She shrugged. "I want to see your bear in more normal circumstances. When it's not busy tearing strips off Tyrell."

He laughed. "Okay then."

Outside, they crossed the stream and Garrett led her into the forest on the far side. When they reached a small clearing, she watched as he stripped, hung his clothes on a tree branch, and shifted gently into his bear form. His bear was beyond excited to be in Savannah's presence, and it stood trembling in front of her. Any seeds of doubt that she would be terrified of it were dispelled when she took a step closer, reached out a hand, and stroked his soft muzzle.

"Beautiful," she breathed. Garrett allowed his bear to take control, and it sniffed her all over, from head to toe. When it tried to push its muzzle between her thighs, she laughed and pushed it away. At last, it touched its giant nose to her tiny one. She stood very still, seeming to understand instinctively that it was important for it to perform this ritual.

When it was satisfied that they had been thoroughly acquainted, Garrett shifted back.

"Does your bear approve of me?" Savannah asked as he pulled his undershorts on. She was a little flushed, but she seemed relaxed.

"Yes. Very much. Too much," he said.

She caught his hand. "Don't look so worried."

He made a noncommittal sound.

"Would falling for me be so bad?" she persisted.

He got a tight feeling in his stomach. "I don't know." He sighed. "I don't trust myself to be close to people, ever since the accident."

Her face turned serious.

"What is it?"

She bit her lip. "Now, I have something to tell you." Immediately, she got very tense, and he could see it was taking a whole lot of effort for her to say what she had to say.

"Tell me. It can't be that bad," he said in a low voice.

"I can't have children anymore." She stared at the ground.

"Because of the accident?"

"Yes," she murmured.

Gently, he reached out with a fingertip and lifted her chin, so she was forced to look at him.

The pain in her eyes broke his heart. He wanted to be with her even more, to protect her from ever feeling so much pain again. "It doesn't matter," he told her. "You're perfect the way you are."

Her eyes got very bright and she blinked fast. "You really mean that?" she whispered. A single tear slid down her cheek.

He leaned forward and caught it with his lips. "Of course, I do. You're the most amazing person I ever met, Savannah."

He drew her into his arms and held her tight. He stroked her back in big, comforting circles, purring softly, until the trembling left her body and she relaxed against him.

She began to run her hands up and down his back, and slowly, her fingertips stoked his desire again. He allowed himself to become aware of the softness of her body against his bare flesh, the press of her breasts against him. Soon, he was slipping off her clothes, and she was tugging at his undershorts. He spread out his clothes on the grass at the side of the tinkling stream, and laid her down on top of them. She looked so beautiful like that, naked in the wild, just the way nature intended. He covered her body with kisses, beginning with her mouth and ending between her thighs. After he'd made her come with his tongue, they had slow, sensual sex. It wasn't the animal passion of the previous time, but deeper and more emotional, as their souls bonded with each other. She kept her eyes open, gazing into his and he felt that she understood him—the only person who ever truly had. She saw his soul and she didn't think he was a monster.

She came again and again, spasming around him so sweetly, and when he orgasmed at last, they lay quietly for a long time, enjoying the sensation of the breeze on their bare skin, the scent of the forest all around.

"I feel like I've just jumped off a cliff without a parachute," he whispered.

She broke into a beautiful smile, her teeth glittering in the sunlight like precious stones. "I won't let you crash," she replied.

CHAPTER 14

Savannah couldn't stop smiling as she opened up the café for the day. She'd just dropped the children off in the library, promising to visit them at break time, and she was about to bake a bunch of new cakes.

She was starting to believe that she and Garrett might have a chance. Yesterday afternoon had been incredible. Beyond incredible. Bonding with his bear had brought her so much closer to him. And then, making love outdoors... Garrett said that it was a special and important thing for shifters to do, and she knew exactly what he meant. It had felt so natural being surrounded by the scent of the wild.

After they'd put the kids to bed, he'd shown her how he'd fixed the door frame, so her bedroom door closed properly, and somehow that had led to them lying down on her bed, then rapidly shedding their clothes. They'd both wanted to spend the night together, and she could tell from his eyes that he was very tempted. But they agreed that it would confuse the children to see him leaving her room. She'd taken a shower in the morning, but she imagined she could still smell him on her. His sexy, masculine scent enveloping her. The memory of his smooth skin, the tender way he held her in his huge arms sent little shivers through her all morning.

She whistled to herself as she worked, gazing out at the beautiful day. The air was crisp and the sky clear blue and cloudless. Whoever had played that matchmaking joke on her might have done her a big favor, after all.

The bells above the café door jingled as someone came in. She sighed. It was Aidan.

He strode across the room and sat down at a table near the counter. "Morning," he said with a nod.

Savannah frowned. Where were the sleazy comments? The endless stream of stupid jokes?

"Morning, Aidan. What can I get you?"

"Just a coffee, please. Americano."

Savannah went to the machine and prepared the coffee, regarding him suspiciously. She brought it over to him. "Do you have a twin?" she demanded.

"Huh?" He looked up from his phone with a polite smile.

She frowned. "You are Aidan, right?"

"The one and only." He winked at her, a hint of his usual swagger returning. "Something wrong, Savannah?"

"Nope. You just seem… different…More mature."

Aidan raised a finger in the air. "Ah!" He fished inside his shirt and pulled out a badge that was on a chain around his neck. It read *Interim Deputy. Ragtown.*

"Very impressive," she said, nodding slowly. "You'll make a good one."

"Thanks for the vote of confidence, Savannah." He smiled, deposited five dollars on the table, and grabbed his coffee. Savannah watched, bemused, as he strode across the room. As he opened the café door, his phone rang, and he answered.

His expression turned serious. "Yup. On my way," he said and picked up his pace.

What was that about? Savannah emptied out the used coffee grounds from the espresso machine and wiped it down.

The café door opened again. Aidan must've forgotten something. She turned to face him.

Her heart leapt into her mouth at the sight of three large, disheveled shifters sidling in. Tyrell and his two sidekicks. Ripe with unwashed wolf stink and bristling with meanness.

Tyrell swaggered over to the counter, as full of himself as always, while there was something malicious and cunning in the eyes of the other two. Savannah's gut tightened, but she worked to keep her expression neutral.

"Good morning," she said in the voice that she used for every other customer. "Today's specialty is Cuban coffee. What can I get for you?"

Tyrell sniggered and the other two joined in. He laid two filthy hands on the counter and looked her up and down deliberately. "Well, so happens we've been looking for a nice piece of ass to breed." He burst into high-pitched laughter, which was immediately echoed by the other two cretins.

Savannah's gut wound another notch. With a gargantuan effort, she attached a professional smile to her face. "Well, I'm afraid I can't have children, so you should go find someone else to harass." She was beginning to tremble all over, but her voice stayed smooth and clear.

Tyrell nodded as if he was seriously considering her advice. "Funny you should say that, because we've been working on a deal with that boyfriend of yours. He says, if we're willing to leave Ragtown for good, he'll hand you over to us as a parting gift. And I've gotta say, that sounds like a fair proposition to me." He licked his lips, nasty eyes lingering on her breasts.

Savannah's anger flared. "My mate wouldn't do that!" she snapped.

Mate? Did that word just slip out of her mouth?

The three of them sniggered, picking up on her discomfort. She cast a glance at the spiral staircase. She needed to get away from those assholes. Maybe she could just walk upstairs calmly and act like nothing was happening?

No. They'd follow her, and no way was she going to expose the children to danger.

"The three of you need to get the hell out of here, right now," she said in the same sweet tone she'd been using all along.

"Oh, I'm not going anywhere, sweetheart." Tyrell darted forward and grabbed her forearm hard enough to make her yelp.

"Get your filthy hands off me!" she hissed.

"Barren or not, you're coming with us. We're going to keep you as our little human prize. Share you around our pack. Maybe sell you on when we've worn you out."

Savannah leaned forward and aimed a slap at his disgusting face. But, still holding onto her, he dodged backward, dragging her body painfully against the counter. He held her there, sneering as she fought to get free. Out of the corner of her eye, she saw the other two slinking around the side of the counter. They were planning to get behind her and…

Fear pulsed through her body. Something very bad was about to happen. Something that would change her life forever. She started to hyperventilate in terror.

A pair of rough hands grasped her hips, and she opened her mouth to scream.

The café door burst open.

There was an earth-shattering roar, and Garrett charged in. "Get off her!" he bellowed.

The wolves released her immediately.

"You've got three seconds to get out of the café, and five minutes to get your asses out of town." The bones in Garrett's face broadened and his body swelled, his clothes getting tight on him. With his huge hands, he grabbed Tyrell and one of the others by the back of the neck and hauled them out of the café. The third one took his cue and tumbled out after them, and Savannah followed, opening the door a crack and peering through. She was worried for Garrett; she'd never seen him looking so mad.

Tyrell was lying in the dirt, glaring at Garrett insolently. "We know all about you, and your past," he spat. "You're a bigger criminal than we are."

Garrett roared again, and his eyes glowed red. His muscles swelled and swelled, and suddenly his bear exploded out of him, his clothes shredded to scraps. It opened its jaws wide and bellowed.

Savannah cowered. He was nothing like the bear she'd met in the forest a few days earlier. This was a terrifying beast, and she was scared that it wouldn't even know her. She clung to the door frame, wanting to lock the door and keep the children and herself safe inside.

But no—he was her mate and their surrogate father. Surely, he wouldn't hurt them?

As she watched in horror, the wolves shifted, too, and Garrett attacked.

This was different from the attack in the park. This time Garrett was fighting to kill, and the wolves didn't stand a chance against him. His claws were merciless, ripping open their hides, their faces. They yelped and screamed and tried to flee. But he was too quick for them. He caught them up again and again in his jaws, hurling them in the dirt, before continuing his assault on them. He wasn't just trying to kill them—he wanted to inflict maximum suffering.

Savannah clapped her hands over her mouth to stop herself from screaming. She'd needed Garrett to save her, but this was too much. Bones were showing through torn flesh; it was a ghastly sight.

Suddenly, Aidan and Jagger came hurtling down the street. At the sight of the carnage, they stopped dead. "Garrett, stop! We can't do this anymore!" Aidan yelled.

But Garrett paid them no heed, and sunk his teeth into Tyrell's muzzle, making the wolf squeal in agony.

The two of them yanked at their clothes, and a huge brown bear and big black wolf burst out of them. Jagger leapt between Garrett and the wolves, up on his back legs, paws raised to stop Garrett's onslaught. But, to Savannah's horror, Garrett swiped at him with his claws, opening a red weal on his face.

Jagger drew back in shock, but Garrett came at him again, jaws open wide, snapping at his muzzle. The wolves abandoned in bloody heaps, Garrett's focus was now on harming his best friend. They were evenly matched in size, but Garrett was less of a bear than a beast that Savannah had no name for. His eyes burned red, and terrible sounds erupted from his mouth as he approached Jagger as if he was the enemy. The fight went on and on, as the bears tumbled to the ground, Jagger fighting defensively, while Garrett looked like he wanted to kill him. At last, Garrett got Jagger on his back, jaws dripping blood and hovering inches above his throat. Savannah gasped. He was really going to do it.

"Garrett!" she screamed. "Stop!"

The beast froze. Then it turned its mighty head in her direction, eyes flickering like embers. There was something so dangerous and dark in there that she thought he was going to kill her, too. Her breath caught in her throat, every nerve in her body desperate to slam the door shut and lock it behind her.

Fat lot of use that would be. He could probably bust it open without even trying. Instead, she stood still, a low keening sound coming from her mouth.

The beast's giant paws crashed onto the ground, either side of Jagger's prone body. It gave her one final dark look, then it leapt over him and galloped away. She yelled his name several more times, but he didn't stop.

The wolves took their cue to escape. As Savannah watched, stiff with horror, they dragged themselves away like snails, leaving trails of blood and gore behind them. Jagger and Aidan shifted back into their human forms and pulled their clothes on. Jagger hissed in discomfort. His flesh was horribly torn and bleeding.

"It's okay now," Jagger told her in a low voice. "It's over."

She discovered that tears were running down her face, and she'd broken out in a cold sweat. "Garrett –?" She broke off not knowing what she was going to say. *Is he okay? Is he going to come back and kill you? Was he really trying to kill you?*

"He'll be fine. He's not going to hurt me," Jagger said intuitively.

She ran her gaze over his blood-soaked shirt. "That's not how it looked from here," she managed to say.

Aidan cocked an eyebrow at her. Luckily, he'd avoided any physical injury. "I warned you about him," he said. "He's more of a beast than the rest of us put together."

"I'd better get home," Jagger indicated his clothes. She nodded, and both of them walked away, leaving her alone on the empty street.

She burst into tears, sobbing into her hands. Now she understood why everyone had been warning her off Garrett—including himself.

CHAPTER 15

Garrett charged through the forest, blood pounding in his veins. He'd almost killed Jagger, his best friend in the world. And he would have, if Savannah hadn't stopped him. Bile rose up in his throat and he stopped and vomited out the horror and shame of the past half hour.

What the hell had he been thinking?

Nothing at all.

That was the truth. His beast had taken over, and all it cared about was killing the wolves. When Jagger had tried to stop him, Jagger had become no more than an obstacle to his objective. His beast had the single-mindedness of a robot. When it had a mission to kill, nothing was going to get in its way. Not friendship…Not love?

What if it had been Savannah standing between him and Tyrell?

He didn't know. And the fact he didn't know filled him with a self-disgust worse than anything he'd felt before.

He ran faster and faster, crashing through the trees. Burning with fury at himself. He knew he shouldn't fall in love with Savannah—because he did love her. He'd known that for a while now. He'd even started to see a future with her. But it didn't take long for the beast in him to come out and trash it all. The look on her face at what he'd done to the wolves was seared into his memory. She was horrified. Disgusted by him. Of course, she was. He should have known better. She was screaming his name when he ran away from the café, and he'd yearned to shift and comfort her as a man. But he'd lost control of his beast, and the only thing he could do was escape to the forest before he killed everyone in sight.

Not Savannah, a small voice said.

Hopefully not Savannah.

He could go back now and speak to her, tell her it wasn't him. He just lost control of his beast because those wolves were attacking her.

No. Speaking to her now was the last thing he should be doing. She probably wanted nothing to do with him ever again. And it was what he deserved.

He ran on and on, aimlessly, seeking out no more than oblivion.

But at last, he started to make for a certain place. It was somewhere he hadn't been to in a long time. The closer he got, the heavier his paws felt, but a force was driving him on, outside of his control.

He reached a small clearing, and when he came to a tall, flat-sided stone, he stopped. He hadn't been able to bring himself to visit it for many months. With the rough pads of his paws, he stroked the surface, where SL was carved into it. Slade's initials. He'd died far away from here, but he knew about Ragtown. He was always talking about how he was going to move there when he quit black ops.

Garrett had moved there partly as a homage to him. And he built him a shrine on the mountain overlooking the town. It was his secret place. No one else knew about it. He hadn't even told the children yet.

He looked down at Ragtown in the valley below and grief washed over him. His bear roared out a wild cry, full of pain, despair and guilt.

***

Savannah

It was long past midnight when Garrett came back to the house. Savannah had brought Poppy, Opal and Holt back from the library, fed them, bathed them and read them a bedtime story. Then, for the past four hours, she'd been sitting at the kitchen table, nursing cups of cocoa and waiting.

He opened the front door quietly and crept in, as if he expected everyone to be sleeping. She heard him pause outside the kitchen, evidently seeing the bar of light beneath the door.

"Come in," she called softly.

He opened the door. He looked terrible. Leaves and twigs were tangled in his cropped hair and his face and arms were covered in dirt and wounds. There were deep shadows beneath his eyes, which were dark and haunted. He was broken and exhausted.

Savannah's heart went out to him. She scraped her chair back, got to her feet and went to him, arms stretched out.

But he pulled away, pain flashing across his face. "You need to leave here," he said, his voice breaking on the final word.

Savannah planted her hands on her hips and shook her head. "I'm not going anywhere, Garrett."

His jaw clenched and his eyes burned like hot coals. "Didn't you see what I did? What I almost did to Jagger? I'm a beast. An uncontrollable beast, unfit to be around humans." He bunched his fists until they went white at the knuckles.

"If you're a beast, then you're my beast," she said. "You saved me from those assholes today. They would've hurt me real bad if you hadn't turned up."

He made a dismissive gesture and hung his head.

"You knew, didn't you?" she continued. "You came because you knew I was in trouble. That your mate was in trouble."

His jaw twitched, but he refused to meet her gaze.

"You need to get out of here. I'm not safe to be around," he muttered.

"We can make everything better," she persisted, wringing her hands. "The two of us."

At last, he lifted his head. His eyes were brimming with emotion. "Savannah, I saw the expression on your face. You were terrified."

She took a step toward him. "Garrett, I was terrified *for* you. Not *because of* you."

He shook his head hard. "That's not true, Savannah. You saw how easy my beast dealt with them. And almost killed Jagger. Who knows what would've happened if you hadn't stopped me."

"Oh, Garrett, I don't believe that. And none of this matters anyway." She reached for his fists, which were still clenched. "What matters is if you love me. We can work through everything else."

But Garrett tore his hands away and turned to the sink, staring out of the window at the inky sky.

Savannah watched him, her throat convulsing. She'd thought… but maybe she'd made a mistake… that he loved her. Didn't he? She didn't want to ask him straight out. Hated the thought. She'd been rejected before, in the worst way, by someone who'd told her that they loved her.

"Do you love me?" Finally, the words erupted from her lips, but quietly. So quietly that she might have thought he hadn't heard her—except for the tell-tale tensing of his shoulders.

She held her breath, staring at the unyielding bulk of his back. *Answer me*, she begged him silently. Tell me now. Tell me anything. Just don't keep me waiting like this. It was a torture. He was holding her beating heart in his hands.

His head turned to the side, but not far enough to look at her. "You should leave in the morning," he said.

She squeezed her eyes shut to stop the tears running down her cheeks. "I'll leave now," she managed to say. She rushed out of the kitchen, heading for the guest room to pack her stuff. Her heart was ripping in two. He didn't love her. That was clear. She pulled her suitcase out from under her bed and began stuffing things into it haphazardly. She wasn't going to give in to tears. She bit down on the end of her tongue, needing the pain to stem her emotions.

When the suitcase was full, she carried it out to the car. The kitchen light was off, and Garrett was nowhere to be seen.

CHAPTER 16

Savannah slumped on the stool behind the counter in the café. It wasn't like her to sit down on the job, but she ached, bone-deep with exhaustion. She didn't think she'd slept at all the previous night. She'd lain on Florence's sofa in the darkness for hours, stomach churning, thinking about Garrett, wishing he felt the same way about her. It was lucky that Florence had woken up when she'd rapped on her door in the middle of the night. She'd been very kind, taking one look at her red eyes and not asking any questions, but offering her a place to stay for as long as she needed it.

Savannah wasn't sure she was going to stay in Ragtown. She couldn't think about anything right now. She just hurt. Garrett hadn't called or come in to the café to see if she was okay. And every time the door opened, she got a pathetic little fizz of hope that it was him. He'd know she was staying with Florence, as that was where she'd stayed before. And he evidently wanted nothing to do with her.

It was so hard being in the café today, when all she wanted to do was hide in bed and cry. She kept replaying that terrible moment when she asked if he loved her and he didn't answer, and each time, her lower lip trembled and her mouth tugged down at the corners, as if she was a puppet, controlled by strings.

Three p.m. came. Soon, he'd come in to collect the children. Maybe if she saw him approaching, she'd have time to go and lock herself in the bathroom until he was gone. But what about tomorrow, and the day after that, and the day after that?

The door opened and a shot of adrenaline charged through her body. It was Ryker. His beard was less straggly than usual, and his hair had recently been cut as well. She plastered a smile to her face and greeted him.

He strode toward her with something approaching a smile. It was weird to see him without a scowl on his face, she noticed distractedly.

"Hi, Savannah. Got the weekly delivery in the truck," he mumbled.

She frowned. "Oh, Florence didn't mention anything?"

He rubbed the back of his head. "Normally, I deliver on Thursdays, but I'm early this week because I've got a thing tomorrow." He cleared his throat. "See, I'm interim deputy sheriff, and Jagger's gonna need me."

Savannah forced a smile. "That's great. Are you competing for the position with Aidan?"

He nodded. "Yes, ma'am."

"Well, good luck. Now, where does the delivery go?"

"I usually leave it in the stockroom." He indicated the small room behind her.

"Okay, great."

"I'll get to it." He saluted her. She watched in bemusement as he went out to his truck. The deputy sheriff position seemed to have transformed Mr. Angry.

Ryker made several trips back and forth, refusing her offers of help.

"Okay, done," he said at last, wiping his hands on his jeans. "I'll sort out payment with Florence later, but I just need to get you to stamp my delivery receipts. Think there's a stamp in the drawer somewhere."

"Oh, okay—" She opened the drawer beneath the till and rooted around. Florence's paperwork was a mess, and the draw was stuffed with random pieces of paper. Eventually she found a stamp, right at the back. But when she pulled it out, a scrap of paper came with it, covered in Florence's messy handwriting. She glanced at it absently, then looked again. It was a list of names: *Ragtown matches; match in Ragtown; Ragtown – match*; then *MateMatch* circled multiple times.

Savannah's breath caught. Ryker was saying something to her, but her thoughts were spiralling everywhere. Florence knew about MateMatch? She'd always denied all knowledge…

"… I'm kind of in a hurry," Ryker was saying. "I can come back later if you haven't found the stamp."

She shook her head. "Got it, sorry." She grabbed the stamp, stamped his papers, and he left.

As soon as he was gone, she snatched up the scrap of paper again. So, Florence didn't just know about the matchmaking agency, but she was actually behind it? This whole time, Florence had pretended to be her friend, offered her partnership in the business. All so she could get her to be the mate of someone who didn't want her? Tears welled up in Savannah's eyes yet again. How could she? She must have known Garrett wasn't looking for a mate. What on earth made her think it was a good plan to drag Savannah all the way up here, only for her to get her heart broken yet again? And then, after Savannah had told her what Garrett had said to her, she persisted, persuading her to stay, when the decent thing would've been to have encouraged her to leave and find a mate someplace far from Ragtown.

She gasped for breath and her legs shook. She sat down heavily, crushed by the weight of the betrayal. It was the final straw.

This town was not for her. It had all been a lie, since the moment she'd arrived. She needed to leave, now. She'd wait until the kids were done with school, and she'd say goodbye to them. But the thought of seeing the kids for the last time broke her heart all over again. She'd started to think of them all as her family. Her instinct was to run away, right now. But she sensed that would hurt them more than anything. So, she'd stay, until they were done with school for the day.

Her stomach was one giant knot as she sat there, counting the minutes.

Four p.m. came and went.

At four-ten p.m., Florence bustled downstairs. "I don't suppose you've seen Garrett this afternoon—?" she broke off at the expression on Savannah's face.

"You lied to me," Savannah hissed. "I know MateMatch is your thing. All those emails you sent me, pretending to be somebody else. All those times you convinced me to hang around, waiting for Garrett, when he obviously wasn't interested." She paused and took deep breaths as a sob racked up in her chest. "How could you do this to me? You know I've been through heartbreak already. Why did you try to set me up with a man who was obviously not available? And why was it all a big secret?"

Florence stared at her, aghast. Her eyes were bulging, and her hair had come loose from her bun and was frizzing around her face, making her look as if she'd been electrocuted. If Savannah wasn't so miserable, she might have found it funny.

"Oh, my dear, I'm so sorry!" Florence blinked rapidly, her eyes turning pink. She tried to reach for Savannah's hands, but Savannah tore them away. "You have to believe I meant well. When you answered my ad, I was so excited, because I thought you were perfect for Garrett. As you know, I care for him and the children so much, and I've been thinking for a long time that he needs to find his mate. He's such a special bear, and I was so sad that he was raising the children alone. That was when I hit on the idea for the matchmaking agency—"

"You created the whole agency because of Garrett?" Savannah cut in.

"Yes, my dear. But in the meantime, I've been thinking that most of the shifters up here would benefit from finding their mate, too."

Savannah closed her eyes, struggling to absorb the information. "But Garrett told you, time and time again, that he wasn't interested in finding a mate. Why did you ignore his wishes?"

Florence threw her hands up. "I know it sounds silly in retrospect, but I could tell he was lonely. And sometimes men need to be convinced that a certain woman is right for them."

Savannah ground her teeth together, then spoke very slowly. "But did you ever stop to think that a certain woman might get hurt in the process? That she might already have had her heart broken, and being rejected by one more guy is more than she can take?"

Tears spilled down Florence's round cheeks. "No, I didn't. And I am heartily sorry for that. I just thought that as soon as Garrett saw you, all his resistance would dissolve. And I can see how much he cares about you, how suited you are to each other. It's obvious to everyone that you're mates."

Savannah jabbed a finger at her. "You obviously didn't know Garrett as well as you thought you did. He's not going to change his mind. I'm done with him. And I'm done with this crappy, screwed-up town." She turned on her heel and marched across the room.

"Savannah! Please, don't go! I'm sure we can work it out. Garrett just needs more time…"

Savannah slammed the door shut, cutting off the end of Florence's sentence. The sooner she got on the road, the better. She hated everything about Ragtown, and the giant lie it had been.

CHAPTER 17

Garrett yanked open the door of the Last Chans Saloon. *Sheesh*, this place was more of a dump than he remembered. It stunk to high heaven and the air was so thick he could almost taste it. Broken beer bottles and peanut shells crunched under his feet as he peered through the murky light, looking for Jagger. There he was, on one of the high stools by the bar. Garrett's gut tightened. Last time they'd seen each other, his beast had been ready to kill him. Garrett kicked aside a half-dozen discarded beer bottles on his way over to him. Instead of the usual bear-hug greeting, he froze, inches away.

"I'm so sorry, brother," he said, hanging his head. "I'll do whatever it takes to make sure it never happens again."

Jagger held his hand up. "Enough. You've apologized plenty already. All of us up here have got problems. We've gotta be understanding when our beasts get crazy."

Garrett groaned. "But you're my best friend. I can't believe I got so out of control."

Jagger shook his big head. "It was a particular situation. I don't think it'll happen again. Now, come here." He held out his arms and gave Garrett his customary rough, backslapping hug.

Garrett's veins flooded with relief. He couldn't stand to lose another friend. He pulled away, his bear purring. "Drink?"

"Yup," Jagger said with a grin, and rapped a fist on the bartop.

Farrell, the bartender, appeared and nodded a hello. He wasn't one to waste words when a gesture would suffice.

"Two beers," Jagger said.

Farrell filled two pint glasses from the bar's only tap and dumped them on the bar. He was always in some kind of mood. No one knew why. In fact, no one really knew anything about the hawk shifter.

Garrett laid a ten and a five on the sticky bar top, and he and Jagger grabbed the beers and dragged two upturned beer crates over to a quiet spot in the corner.

Jagger's huge jaw was set in a hard line. "The time we gave the wolves to clear out of town is up, and they still haven't left," he said, regarding Garrett seriously through the gloom.

Garrett adjusted his position on the uncomfortable seat. "Has anyone seen them since yesterday? Are they still in one piece?"

Jagger gave a dry laugh. "After the way they dragged their asses off, bleeding all over the road? They're lucky you didn't put them down. You were well within your rights to."

Garrett cocked an eyebrow. He'd already been thinking the same thing: it would have been so much easier if he'd taken them out in the heat of the moment. He wasn't the kind of guy who could go and kill them in cold blood, however much he wanted to.

"I went past their house on patrol last night, and it sounds like they're still alive and kicking," Jagger continued. They must be scared, though. If they've got any sense."

Garrett snorted. "Sense is something that's in short supply when it comes to them. Knowing them, they're probably plotting revenge."

"I vote we drive them out of town today."

"Yeah, good idea," Garrett said absently.

Jagger's hand landed on his shoulder. "Bro, you seem kind of distracted."

Garrett shook his head, trying to clear his thoughts. "I'm okay."

Jagger's big brown eyes narrowed. "Like hell you are. It's Savannah, isn't it?"

Savannah. At the sound of her name, Garrett's bear howled inside him. She was all he'd been thinking about since…well, since she'd first arrived on his doorstep, really, looking sexy and vulnerable and tough, all rolled into one.

He'd been dumb enough to think he could stop her from getting under his skin. That she could be nothing more than a nanny to his kids. What a joke. He let off a snort. His attraction to her had grown every day, until he needed to be with her more than he needed his next breath.

"Uhh, Garrett? You okay?"

Garrett's head snapped in Jagger's direction. The big bear looked worried. "Savannah and I are over. I was stupid to think I could be normal and have a relationship. All I've done is end up hurting her. It's best we don't see each other again."

Jagger's expression got very serious. "Garrett, listen to me. When a woman is your mate, the worst pain you can cause her is not being with her. You're probably tearing her apart, in a way she might never recover from."

Garrett clawed at his forearms, his bear fretting and pacing beneath his skin. "I'm not worthy of her. The sooner she forgets about me, the better."

"You've got to stop punishing yourself for what happened with Slade. It was an accident. We talked about this a hundred times, and I'm happy to discuss it a hundred more, until you believe that."

Garrett groaned. "It might have been an accident, but it turned me into a beast."

"Isn't that what mates are for—to tame the beast?" Jagger swigged his beer, watching him shrewdly over the rim.

"But she didn't tame the beast. If anything, protecting her has turned me into more of a beast."

Jagger snorted. "She stopped you from taking half my face off, dude. If that's not taming, then what is?"

Garrett stared into his beer. "She's a tough one, all right. Strong, determined, committed. That's why she needs a perfect mate, not a broken bear."

Jagger shrugged. "I'd say a perfect mate is one who'd do anything for her, And I can tell by the look in your eyes that you would. Garrett, do us all a favor and go speak to her."

Garrett finished his beer and dumped the glass on the floor. "She's left and she isn't coming back."

"Then go after her. Maybe you can change her mind. You won't know until you try."

Garrett fell silent, his head too full with conflicting thoughts. The truth was, he was broken without her. He thought he'd feel better after she left, and she was safely away from the beast that he was. But he didn't. He felt as miserable as he'd ever been.

He stood up abruptly, slapping Jagger on the knee. "I've gotta go. Thanks for the chat."

GARRETT SPRINTED down the high street, kicking up a huge cloud of dust. When he got to the library, he yanked the door open and burst in.

Florence was pacing up and down the café, face contorted with worry.

Panic charged through his veins. "Where are the kids?" he demanded.

"They're napping," she said, indicating the upper floor.

But his panic didn't recede. A sense of impending disaster turned his blood cold. "And Savannah?"

Florence's misery mirrored his own. "She's gone. For good. And it's my fault." She wrung her hands together. "I was only trying to help. I just thought you two would be so perfect together—"

But she didn't get to complete her sentence, because Garrett was sprinting out of the café. "Please watch the kids," he yelled over his shoulder.

Savannah must be heading down the mountain road. And it was

going to be dark way before she made it onto the highway. He had to go after her. He sprinted all the way back to his house to collect his pickup.

But when he arrived, he stopped dead. Savannah's battered red sedan was still there. Adrenaline lurched through his chest. He bounded up the front steps and through the front door, shouting Savannah's name.

It took less than five seconds to discover that she wasn't there. *Then where the hell was she?* He stood in the kitchen, staring blankly out of the window at the darkening sky. If she hadn't left Ragtown, then where could she be? Florence wasn't hiding her—there was too much guilt and shame showing on her face. With Timon? One of the other guys? It was possible. But it just didn't feel right. He knew she was too cautious to be alone with them.

He left the house and paced up and down the dirt road, waiting for an idea to strike him.

CHAPTER 18

Savannah was sitting on the far bank of the stream, watching the cold water meander along. The mercury was dropping fast and it would soon be dark, but she didn't care. She'd meant to leave Ragtown, but it turned out that she didn't even have the energy to get into her car.

She'd thought she knew loneliness, but this was a whole other level. Being rejected by her first mate had hurt like hell, but she felt ten times more for Garrett than she'd ever felt for Joel. She'd fallen hard for the big bear, and he had torn her heart to shreds. All because of that stupid Florence and her meddling ways.

Savannah had barely been surviving before she came to Ragtown. And now, her future was even bleaker. She knew she wouldn't make it past this heartbreak alive. She took her phone out of her back pocket and switched it on. It beeped with an array of messages. It was the first time she'd turned it on since she'd spoken to Joel. Every single message was from him, begging her to come back. He'd made a terrible mistake. He'd do whatever it took to make her happy. There was even a surrogate lined up who was willing to have their babies.

She squeezed her eyes shut and bit down on her lower lip, but tears spilled down her cheeks regardless.

Knowing Garrett had made her realize what a horrible, spineless loser her ex was. Garrett was everything Joel wasn't—passionate protective and caring. He might have pushed her away, but he never set out to hurt her. Meanwhile, her ex never cared about her feelings, only his own. No way was she going back to him. He didn't deserve her, she knew that, and her heart still belonged to Garrett, even though he didn't want her.

Behind her, the long grasses rustled. Her head whipped around. Garrett. Silhouetted in the darkness. She'd know him anywhere. "What are you—?" she began.

"I'm sorry," he said, his voice raw with regret as he fell to his knees beside her. He looked sadder and more broken than ever. "I love you, Savannah. I knew you were my mate since the moment I laid eyes on you. My bear knew, too. I was just scared to listen to it, because I thought it would only hurt you. But I know you can pacify it. You were the one that stopped it from killing Jagger. It's only calm when we're together."

Savannah clapped a hand over her mouth. "I can't take any more heartbreak, Garrett," she whispered when she was able to speak.

He shook his head wordlessly. "No heartbreak. I want to be with you always. Please don't leave Ragtown. Please stay with me and be my mate." His voice broke and his eyes filled with anguish.

"Do you mean this?" she said in a quavering voice.

"Of course, I do, Savannah. I know how serious this is." Garrett reached for her hands, but she sat frozen. "We've both had a tough time in life, but I know we can face our problems together."

"If I say yes, there can't be any more back and forth." She sat up straight and regarded him seriously. "No more running. If you're offering to be my mate, then you'd better mean it. You can't wake up in a month's time, or a year's time, and realize you want to have more kids."

Garrett shook his head slowly. "I just want you, Savannah. I have kids already. And I know you love them, too. All I want is to share my life with you, in a happy home. Even if I didn't have kids, you'd be more than enough for me."

Her lips parted in a gasp, but she didn't trust herself to speak.

"I want to give you my mate mark. And a bear never goes back on that. I don't know what codes wolves live by, but to us, it means forever."

"Forever?" she breathed.

"Forever and beyond," he said solemnly.

Smiling through her tears, Savannah got up and threw herself into his arms. She fit against him so perfectly, her legs wrapping around his waist, arms around his neck, his huge arms enfolding hers, and the lips she thought she'd never kiss again searing hers.

It was a passionate but tender kiss, full of everything that had been unsaid between them. It went on and on, neither of them wanting to break away, but eventually, the touch of his tongue became insistent, and his cock grew hard, pressing against her crotch through both sets of clothing.

Slowly, reverently, he began to unbutton her shirt. Her bra followed and she sat astride him, topless. When his big hands covered her breasts, she moaned, desire charging through her body. She got to her feet and slipped off her jeans, followed by her panties. It was almost dark now, but she sensed he could see her, that he was drinking her in. He stripped off, too, and laid her down on a bed of his clothing, then he arched over her, huge and powerful and protective. When he began to enter her, she cried out and pulled him close, eager for him to be inside her. With a purr of pleasure, he slid all the way in, filling her with his girth.

He held her in his arms, kissing her constantly as he thrust in and out, setting her insides on fire. It was hot and wild, but very romantic. When his head dipped to her throat, she bared it to him, knowing what was coming. Knowing what they both needed.

His teeth were gentle, gentler than she'd expected, but he didn't let go. He kept up the pressure as he buried himself deep inside her, the powerful rhythm of his thrusts working her up into a powerful orgasm. As her climax approached, she trembled all over and gripped him tight, and when she tipped over the edge, he climaxed too, shooting his seed deep inside her.

"That was it?" she asked, minutes later, touching at her neck. The flesh wasn't broken, but it felt hot, and there were definite ridges.

"That was it," he said with a laugh, his eyes glittering in the darkness. "You're mine now, and there's no escape. Forever."

She shivered deliciously. That felt like heaven. "I love being yours, Garrett," she murmured.

"And I love you." He kissed her on the nose. "I can't wait to spend all our time together, getting to know each other better."

"Me, too—" she broke off, as an anxious thought jolted her.

Garrett frowned and stroked her cheek. "What is it, baby?"

"But what about the kids? Will they be okay with this?"

He laughed in relief. "I think they'll be very okay. They've wanted us to get together ever since they first barged into the bedroom and saw you sleeping on that first day."

Savannah caught his hand and held it. "That's so good to hear. I'd love to take care of them all the time. I mean, I'll never replace their mom, but—"

"And I'll never replace their dad. But together, I think we'll do a pretty decent job of raising them."

Savanna's eyes filled with tears. She felt like she was dreaming. She'd felt like her life was over. And now she had her forever mate, and the three best kids anyone could ask for. Her heart felt like it was going to burst with happiness. She wiped her tears away and sat up, looking for her clothes.

"Somewhere you need to be?" Garrett said teasingly.

"Shall we go and give them the news?" she said.

Garrett sat up as well, took her face in his strong hands and kissed her on the lips. "I can hardly wait."

EPILOGUE

There was a huge grill in the backyard, laden with freshly-hunted meat, while three glowing braziers warded off the late-October chill. As darkness fell, a witch, a ghost and a vampire raced around, chasing each other and hunting for treats. A barbecue wasn't the most conventional way of celebrating Halloween, but Savannah and Garrett had decided it was a sensible alternative to trick-or-treating around Ragtown. It was the kids' first Halloween, and they were having a lot of fun. Savannah had decorated the yard and hidden candy all over it. Their guests, Jagger, Ryker, Brock, Callan and Timon had also brought treats, which they handed out in exchange for the kids entertaining them with magic tricks and acrobatic feats.

Garrett gazed at the scene, taking a moment to appreciate all he had. Timon was doing a great job cooking the food, while Jagger was setting it out on plates. Ryker was explaining to Callan, yet again, that the wolves had abandoned their house and left town for good, while Brock had all three children safely occupied, by pretending to be a mountain and letting them climb all over him.

Garrett went over to Savannah, who'd been soft and dreamy all evening. He stood behind her and slipped his arms around her waist. "How are you feeling?" he murmured, nuzzling her soft, sweet-smelling neck.

"In shock." She laughed quietly. "Definitely in shock. But so, so happy."

He leaned around her and kissed her on the lips. Then he ran his hands over her soft belly. "I can't believe there's a little bear in there."

She laid her hands on his. "Me neither. It's a miracle. Our miracle."

He'd felt she was pregnant for two months now, but neither of them could believe it after what the doctors had told her. Then, the previous day, they'd driven down the mountain to see a shifter doctor that Florence had recommended. They got the news this morning—Savannah was definitely pregnant, and the fetus was strong and healthy. He'd never expected to have cubs of his own, and when Savannah had shared that she couldn't have children, it hadn't bothered him one bit. But now the news that he was going to be a father filled him with pride and excitement. His bear wouldn't quit purring.

As they stood in each other's arms, whispering to each other, a white-sheeted ghost bounded up to them, eyes blinking behind two cut-out eye holes. "Are you having a baby?" it demanded.

Garrett suppressed a sound of surprise. He rubbed the ghost's head. "What gives you that idea, Squirt?" he asked innocently.

Behind the eye cut-outs, he could just make out an eye roll. "Durr…because it's obvious," Holt said

Garrett frowned. "Obvious, how?"

"We can feel it, because we're bears," Holt said in a patient tone.

Garrett and Savannah burst out laughing.

Savannah reached out and put an arm around the little ghost. "It's true, I'm pregnant, and you'll have a new brother or sister in six months' time."

Holt let out a yell, then the witch and the vampire hurried over on their little legs.

"Are we having a new sister?" the vampire demanded.

Garrett laughed. So much for keeping things quiet until they were sure about the pregnancy. It seemed like the kids had known all along.

"Maybe it's a brother," the witch shrilled. "I wouldn't mind either."

Garrett chuckled to himself.

"Can I touch the baby?" Holt asked.

"Of course!" Savannah lifted up the sheet that was covering Holt and reached for his hand. She laid it flat against her belly. "It's too early to feel it kick, but it's in there, growing a little every day."

Holt pressed his face close to her belly. "I can't wait to meet you, little one," he whispered. Savannah's eyes stung with tears. There had been a tiny seed of worry that the kids wouldn't appreciate having a baby around, that they'd feel sidelined in some way. But they were obviously as excited as she and Garrett were.

"If it's a girl, can we call her Rapunzel?" Poppy demanded.

"Maybe if she's born with really, really long hair," Savannah said, laughing.

"Let's call her Honey," Opal suggested.

Garrett nodded seriously. "Honey is a good name. But since it's the name of one of your favorite foods, she'll never know whether you're calling for her or your lunch."

Opal sighed dramatically. "Guess you've got a point."

"Let's call her Ariel from *The Little Mermaid*," Poppy said.

Savannah and Garrett exchanged glances.

"I love it," Savannah said, and Garrett agreed.

"But it might be a boy," Garrett added hurriedly, before they got too sold on the idea.

"If it's a boy you could call it Garrett?" Holt said.

Garrett's breath caught in his throat and he felt as if he'd been punched.

Holt pulled off the sheet and stared up at him earnestly. The kid didn't need to say anything; Garrett knew what he was thinking.

"That's a real nice idea, Holt," he said, struggling to keep his voice even. "But what about Slade, like your real father?"

Holt fell silent. "Okay, maybe Garrett Slade, or Slade Garrett."

"They both sound like nice options," Garrett said. Holt grinned, satisfied, and pulled the sheet over his head again. As the kids continued to discuss other names for future babies, he and Savannah slipped away and left them to it.

"I'm so happy," Savannah said. "You're amazing, Garrett, you know that? You've made the impossible happen."

He hugged her, tenderly. "We both did. I think it's because we're fated to be together."

A loud *hellooo!* came from the front of the house.

"Back here, Florence!" Garrett yelled. He grinned as a short, curvy figure with wild red hair appeared around the side of the house. "Looking forward to giving Florence the news?" he muttered to Savannah.

She laughed. "Sure am. She'll be ecstatic. She's been making a bunch of adverts for all the other guys in town."

Garrett chuckled. "Well, I would've said there's no chance. But I no longer doubt her abilities."

"Me neither. I can't wait to find out who she matches next." Savannah turned and drew him down for a kiss.

"She'll have a job on her hands, that's for sure." Automatically, they looked in the direction of the other guys. Ryker was going on one of his rants about how Ragtown needed a bigger law office, while Jagger was tapping a pair of cooking tongs against his own head in boredom, and Timon looked like he was desperate to escape the conversation and go hide up a tree. Brock and Callan were standing off to one side, getting a little snarly with each other. Brock had his arms wrapped around his body—a sure sign that he was fighting to subdue his lion, while Callan was issuing warning puffs of smoke from his nostrils. It seemed impossible that any of these beasts would be suited to cohabiting with a female. And yet...

Garrett stroked her hair. "Savannah, thank you for giving this broken bear a chance. For turning it into the happiest bear in the world."

"You're very welcome," she said against his lips. "You were a difficult old bear sometimes, but I knew you were worth it, every step of the way. I was never going to give up on you."

"And that's why I love you so much," he murmured.

THE END

THANK YOU!

Hi, I'm excited to share my mail-order bride series with you, and I really hope you enjoyed this first book! If so please consider leaving a review; even if it's only a line or two, it will be greatly appreciated. <3

There are five more books in the series. You can get them on my website at arianahawkes.com/matematch-outcasts.

Also! In case you didn't know, I have a complete **15-book totally binge-worthy matchmaking series** available. It features Shiftr, the secret dating app that helps curvy girls and sexy shifters find their happy ever after! Many of the books have been bestsellers - and my readers tell me that Shiftr is their favourite app yet! ;-) Visit arianahawkes.com/shiftr to start your journey! :-)

If you like to be notified of new releases, sign up for my mailing list at arianahawkes.com/mailinglist. You can also follow me on BookBub at bookbub.com/authors/ariana-hawkes

Thanks again for reading – and for all your support!

Yours,

— ARIANA

READ THE NEXT BOOK IN THE SERIES

Protector Mate (MateMatch Outcasts Book 2)

★★★★★ "When these two meet its **fireworks in more than one way**. This book has it all - **humor, romance, danger and hot sensual moments**; and best of all, **a fantastic HEA**."

★★★★★ "**Absolutely Amazing!** So full of **exciting twists and turns** that you will not see coming."

Jagger needs a mate. Fast. He's running from a dark past and his life as the self-appointed sheriff of the outcast community of Ragtown was supposed to keep him on track. But his duties are pushing his bear to the dark side—not least when a new threat appears in town, with the ability to destroy everyone in it. He needs a woman to stabilize the beast in him, before the animal has turned into one of the criminals he's trying to pursue. But smart, feisty Rowan is not what Jagger expected.

Get at arianahawkes.com/matematch-outcasts

SHIFTR: SWIPE LEFT FOR LOVE - BOOK 1 (DINA)

The original best-selling dating app series, relaunched for summer 2020!

What if your fated mate was just an app swipe away?

Immerse yourself in the loves and adventures of sassy girls and sexy shifters as Shiftr, the **secret dating app**, helps them find their happy ever after. There are **fifteen books in the series**. Visit arianahawkes.com/shiftr to begin your exciting journey with the paw-print dating app!

★★★★★ "**Shiftr is one of my all-time favorite series**! The stories are funny, sweet, exciting, and scorching hot! And they will **keep you glued to the pages!**"

★★★★★ "**I wish I had access to this app**! Come on, someone download it for me!"

Curvy Dina hates the idea of online dating. But her best friend Lauren has a secret she's bursting to share: there are men out there who absolutely love voluptuous girls like her. All Dina has to do is tap Shiftr, the cute little paw-print app that Lauren has just installed on her phone…

Get at arianahawkes.com/shiftr

ALSO BY ARIANA HAWKES

Shifter Dating App Romances
Shiftr: Swipe Left for Love – Book 1
Shiftr: Swipe Left for Love – Books 2-5
Shiftr: Swipe Left for Love – Books 6-8
Shiftr: Swipe Left for Love – Books 9-12
Shiftr: Swipe Left for Love – Books 13-15

MateMatch Outcasts
Grizzly Mate (MateMatch Outcasts Book 1)
Protector Mate (MateMatch Outcasts Book 2)
Rebel Mate (MateMatch Outcasts Book 3)
Monster Mate (MateMatch Outcasts Book 4)
Dragon Mate (MateMatch Outcasts Book 5)
Wild Mate (MateMatch Outcasts Book 6)

Fire Trails (Reverse harem romance)
In collaboration with K.N. Knight
Of Ashes And Sin (Fire Trails Book 1)
Queen Of Ashes (Fire Trails Book 2)

Shifterhood
Tiger's Territory (Shifterhood Book 1)

In Dragn Protection
Ethereal King (In Dragn Protection Book 1)
Boreas Reborn (In Dragn Protection Book 2)
Wounded Wings (In Dragn Protection Book 3)

Broken Hill Bears

Bear In The Rough (Broken Hill Bears Book 1)

Bare Knuckle Bear (Broken Hill Bears Book 2)

Bear Cuffs (Broken Hill Bears Book 3)

Christmas Bear Shifter Romances

Winter Bearland

Hill Bear Christmas

Three Shifter Christmas

Ultimate Bear Christmas Magic Box Set

Bear All I Want For Christmas Boxed Set

Bear Home For Christmas

Bear Christmas Magic

Bear My Perfect Gift

Polar Bears' Christmas

Standalone books

Lost To The Bear

Ravished by the Ice Palace Pack

Your free book is waiting!

A 4.5-star rated, comedy romance featuring one kickass roller derby chick, two scorching-hot Alphas, and the naughty nip that changed their lives forever.

The only thing missing from Aspen Richardson's life is a man who will love her just the way she is. In the small town she calls home, bullies from the past remain, making her wonder if it's ever going to happen. But, things are about to change in a major way, as the secret Aspen's parents have been keeping from her comes out...

"This book definitely needs to be added to your MUST read list – you will quickly fall in love with this steamy and fast paced story."

Get your free book at arianahawkes.com/freebook

ABOUT THE AUTHOR

USA Today bestselling author Ariana Hawkes writes spicy romantic stories with lovable characters, plenty of suspense, and a whole lot of laughs. She told her first story at the age of four, and has been writing ever since, for both work and pleasure. She lives in Massachusetts with her husband and two huskies.

Sign up for updates at arianahawkes.com/mailinglist.

www.facebook.com/arianahawkes
www.twitter.com/arianahawkes
ariana@arianahawkes.com

Made in the USA
Monee, IL
06 April 2024